Secret Baby For My Best Friend's Brother

Callie Stevens

Chapter 1

Jackson

"I'm hiring a stylist," Gemma says, and I look up from the notebook I'm scribbling lyrics in.

"A stylist? Why?" I ask. We've always worn whatever we wanted, and we certainly hadn't had a stylist on tour.

"Because you all look like a bunch of Nirvana rejects, that's why," Gemma explains dryly.

I shake my head, smiling a little. "Don't pull punches on account of me," I joke.

"We need a more cohesive style for this next concert. I know you've been focused on the new album, and I'm proud of you, but Jack and the Spades needs to ride this popularity high for as long as we can," my sister continues.

"It's not my fault we ended up taking two breaks from touring and only did the gigs. Blame that on Locke and Axel, they're the fertile ones," I scoff. "You don't catch *me* getting anyone pregnant with a rug rat."

Cain rolls over on his blanket on the floor and squeals at me, as if reminding me that I love the little rug rat.

I coo at him and go over to pick him up, sitting him on my knee as I write. He grabs at my pen and kicks around.

"Fine. Do you have anyone in mind?" I ask, and Gemma grins.

"Yeah, actually. My best friend from high school, remember her?"

I vaguely remember a mousy, petite girl who used to hang around Gemma all the time, but barely.

"Sure," I lie, and Gemma rolls her eyes.

"Susie Carmichael, remember?"

"Sure," I say again, although the name doesn't ring any bells.

"She goes by her middle name now, Zoe," Gemma says, and I freeze.

Zoe isn't exactly an uncommon name, I suppose, but it still stings to think about the girl I met while we were on tour.

Meeting a girl on tour that I connected with more than any other woman wasn't something that I expected, but here I am. I tried and tried to convince Gemma to stay in Albuquerque another couple of days, but the tour had to go on, and luckily, my blue-haired goddess Zoe followed suit.

So, I snuck around the entire tour, sneaking Zoe into my hotel rooms, stealing kisses at breakfast before the others got up, picking her up on the sink in dirty club bathrooms. She deserved better, and I wanted to give that to her.

She bit down on her bottom lip when I asked her to come to Tucson and for us to make a real go of it.

"We've got a good thing going now, Jackson. We have fun together, don't we?"

I'd swayed toward her, not drunk on tequila but on her, the way she smelled like cherry blossoms and whiskey. I tried to put my arms around her waist but she backed away, into the elevator.

"Yeah, we have fun, but what if it's more than that, Zoe? What if we could be good together? Give me your number, at least."

Zoe was standing in the elevator, about to go up to her room, and she gave me a sly smile.

"You wouldn't call me," she said, and pressed the button. I stared at her until the doors closed, and she kept that sly smile.

So, I don't have her number, or even her last name. We hooked up over half a dozen times on tour, but she didn't give me any identifying information. The only thing I know is that her name is Zoe, and she has a four-year-old son who I'd met only twice, while we were in Dallas.

His name is Elijah and he's smart as a whip, and adorable, too, just like her. He has her dark hair, and he likes music, too, and classic rock, of all things. I never considered dating a single mom, but Elijah is something else and it makes me wonder. I'm nearing thirty and all my friends are having kids, so maybe someone like Zoe would be good for me, would help me to settle down without having to have a kid of my own.

It hadn't been just a fling for me, and I tried to tell her that the last night, but she'd gone up in the elevator and out of my life as if it meant nothing at all.

I frown down at my notebook, thinking of how I needed a sultry female voice to sing the backup lines, and remembering Zoe's sweet, alto tone when she had sung along with my songs.

"Jack?"

I shake my head, ridding myself of thoughts of Zoe. My Zoe and this Zoe are two different people, after all, and I need to focus on the band and on our music. Maybe it's for the best that we didn't end up hooking up back at home.

I know I have the tendency to fall hard, and I don't need to be distracted right now, since the Spades are going on their second national tour.

We're starting in Santa Fe, this time, with Axel's return from paternity leave, and being close to our hometown should mean that there's a *lot* of fans. Gemma's right: we need a stylist to give us something unique.

"Sorry. Just thinking about the album," I say, even though that's partially a lie.

"What's wrong?"

I shake my head. "Nothing. I just haven't found a backup singer just yet."

Gemma frowns slightly, and I can almost see the wheels turning in her head. She's frugal when it comes to spending the band's money, so I'd planned to hire someone for just a few hours a week to do the backup lines out of my own pocket.

"So, when are you gonna hire her?" I ask, changing the subject, and Gemma smirks.

"I already did."

"You weren't even gonna run it by me?" I ask, and Gemma pouts a little.

"I just did."

Damn, my sister is hardheaded. Strong-willed is an understatement, and sometimes, I feel sorry for my best friend for having married her. She's a great girl, but she doesn't listen.

I chuckle, shaking my head. "Fair enough. When does she start?"

"Tonight," Gemma says simply. "We have a gig tomorrow, so we need someone right away, right?"

"And the fact that she's your best friend doesn't have anything to do with this, right?"

Gemma frowns. "No, not really. I haven't talked to her in years, after all. We lost touch after high school. I saw her again in the supermarket and asked her what she was up to. Remember, she was already interested in design when we were kids."

I nod as if I remember, but to be honest, I don't. I was kind of a mess back then. After all those years of abuse our parents had put us through, their death was at the same time a bit of a relief and added pressure. Barely out of high school, I now had to grieve my abusive parents and support myself and my little sister. Not that that was much different than before. I was always trying to find odd jobs since I was about twelve to make sure both me and Gemma had something to eat most days, since all my parents cared about was where to find their next hit, be it booze or drugs. I had to become an adult really fucking fast and my sister, as always, depended on me. Except now, I was all she had. Those were difficult times and there was a lot going on, so everything was sort of a haze.

"She's coming to meet everyone tonight at dinner, so you better be there." Gemma points at me, pulling me out from my trip down shitty memory lane.

Bossy.

I know better than to say that, though. "Sure, I'll be there. The diner?"

"Where else?" Gemma grins. The diner was her favorite place to get all her pregnancy cravings met, and she still seems to have the same tastes. French toast and French onion soup seem like an odd combination to me, but what do I know?

"All right, now get out," Gemma demands, and I blink at her.

"You're kicking me out?"

"Yep. Zoe's coming over so we can ride together, and I don't want you distracting her."

I stare at her blankly. "Why would I distract her?"

Gemma rolls her eyes. "You really don't remember her, do you? She never said anything, but the way she sometimes looked at you, I could swear she had the *biggest* crush on you when we were growing up."

I grin. "Oh?"

"Don't you dare." Gemma points at me again. "You keep it in your pants, Jackson Arden, or I swear to God—"

"Okay, okay!" I laugh. I don't have any designs on Gemma's friends, anyway. I'm still reeling from meeting *my* Zoe and hoping that I'll see her blue hair somewhere in the crowd at the concert tomorrow.

I stand up, sliding my notebook into my back pocket, and that's when a car pulls up in the driveway.

I don't pay any attention, looking around for my keys, until I hear a small squeak.

When I look up, there's a blue-haired goddess standing in our garage.

My face goes pale. She looks pale, also, rubbing a hand across the back of her neck.

"Hello, Jackson."

My Zoe is Gemma's Zoe.

What the *fuck?*

Chapter 2

Zoe

I'm stupid.

This is a well-known fact to me, but I'm *particularly* stupid about Jackson Arden, and I lose all rational thought when he's in my general vicinity. It's been that way since I was fifteen and I had a huge crush on my best friend's brother, and it extended to now, at twenty-two, as well.

The thing about Jackson Arden is that he's one of the most responsible people I've ever met, while also being the biggest mess I've ever met. He takes care of his little sister, Gemma, my best friend, like she's his own daughter, even though he's only a few years older than her. He must have been just as devastated as Gemma after his parents' death, but he'd stepped up to take care of her, done everything that he could to raise her right, while also hard partying while working two or three jobs to support them.

There's this maturity in him that has always been fascinating to me. He's the only guy I've ever met who was like that, and it attracted me immediately. I guess some things never change.

I already knew that I am still stupid about Jackson, given that he'd winked at me *once* at the first concert I'd seen him at back in Dallas and I'd ended up in his hotel room the next morning. Then I'd done it *again*, taking him to my place, which was extra stupid given that my babysitter brought Elijah back too early the next morning.

I'd been terrified of them meeting, of course, terrified that Jackson would notice something, but he hadn't. He'd been good with Elijah, singing along to The Who when Elijah showed him his little Walkman that I'd bought him..

Elijah and Jackson had their music taste in common, and many other things as well. Elijah had his eyes and his smile, too, because Elijah is *his*.

When Jackson hit on me in Dallas, at first, I was offended that he didn't recognize me, but I'd grown up from the seventeen-year-old girl with a crush.

I still remember the first thing he said to me that night.

"Susie, you're prettier than you think, you know?" He had let go and was pretty drunk, swaying on his feet.

Blushing, I put both hands on his chest to steady him. "Yeah? You've never noticed before."

His green eyes were bloodshot and hazy, but still beautiful when he looked down at me, grabbing my wrists with his hands when I tried to pull away.

"I'm noticing now."

He leaned down, and when his lips touched mine, I was lost.

I'd been lost since the moment we met when I was fifteen, if I was honest with myself, and now he was standing in front of me, frowning. Something like anger flashed in his green eyes and I licked my lips, my throat suddenly dry.

"Hello, Jackson."

He doesn't respond and Gemma nudges him with her shoulder.

Jackson sighs, not quite looking at me. "Hello, *Susie.*"

Shit. He *is* mad. So what, I didn't tell him who I was when we first hooked up at the concert. Why would I? He didn't remember me, and I should have been pissed off enough not to hook up with him, but like I already established, I'm stupid about Jackson Arden, and I guess I always will be.

Besides, *I'm* the one who should be mad. At him. At what had happened years ago. And now, what, he's ashamed of me? Because I'm Gemma's friend?

I set my jaw, speaking through gritted teeth. "Good to see you again, Jackson," I say, and he nods before excusing himself to leave the garage, jumping in the same car he's had since high school.

It isn't like I didn't know I would have to see him again, but I was hoping he didn't react like *this.*

"What's his problem?" Gemma asks, and I shrug.

"How should I know? I just got here and he's *your* brother," I say shrugging, feigning ignorance. Because I do know. But I don't want to talk about it now.

Jackson has always been friendly and outgoing, which is one of the reasons I'd fallen for him. He's a natural flirt.

Gemma frowns but takes my hand, dragging me inside. "This is Cain," she says proudly, pointing at the baby rolling around on a blanket.

I grin, crouching down to look at him. "This is such a good age. Hi, big boy!"

Cain squeals up at me and I feel a pang in my heart, thinking of Elijah at this age.

"You've got one, too, right?" Gemma says. "Maybe we could have a playdate."

My smile fades. "Maybe. Elijah is a little older."

I'm being vague on purpose. Gemma is a lot more observant than Jackson.

Gemma waves a hand dismissively. "It'll be fine. Cain's a rough and tumble guy, aren't you, sweetie?"

Cain shouts something incoherent and Gemma laughs.

"He's a lot louder than his father. Gets it from me."

"Locke Kincaid, huh?" I ask, smiling at Gemma, and she has the grace to blush a little.

She shrugs. "What can I say? I guess I have a thing for older guys."

I snort. "Well, good for you."

Gemma and I hadn't stayed in touch after graduation. I had left town and never returned until now. I regret it. It's great seeing how happy she is, how she's squeezing my hand. It's good to have my best friend back, even if her brother is trouble for me.

"I figured we should start with Jackson, first," Gemma says, and I stiffen.

"Jackson? Why? He's pretty stylish."

"If you call ripped jeans and holey T-shirts stylish," Gemma groans. "Jack and the Spades have the whole grunge thing going on, and that's fine, but I want to find a way to make them come together more, you know?"

I nod, understanding exactly what she means. "Yeah, even if it's a casual style, you want them to kind of match."

Gemma gives me a bright smile. "Exactly." She pauses and then pulls me into a hug. She's a little taller than me so she rests her head on my shoulder. "I'm glad to have you back, Suze."

"Zoe," I remind her, and she shakes her head.

"That's going to take just a little getting used to. Be patient with me."

I smile. "I will, no worries. So, we need to go shopping?" I ask, and Gemma's face falls.

"We do, but I can't go with you," she says mournfully. "I don't have anyone to watch the kiddo and he's a holy terror in public. I'm still breastfeeding," she explains.

My eyes widen. "Good for you. Elijah got teeth at four months, and I gave it up," I admit.

Gemma winces. "I'm glad I don't have to deal with that, just yet. Axel's wife says their little girl is already teething and she's a couple months older than Cain."

"Everyone's having babies," I muse, and Gemma nods.

"Everyone but Jackson."

My mouth goes dry again. I want to tell Gemma about me and Jackson, but I can't. It's been years since we were best friends, so I just swallow the lump in my throat and remember once again ,that I'm playing with fire taking this job because he most definitely *does* have a baby, it's just that no one knows about it. And I don't want anyone to find out.

But: A. I need a job. Badly. I've been working as a waitress for four years now, and it's just not paying the bills. I've had to move back to New Mexico to stay with my parents because of my lack of funds. Designing is what I've always wanted to do, and this would be a step in the right direction. And B. I'm still stupid about Jackson Arden.

After we had our little fling on tour and he was so sweet and earnest, asking me if I wanted to come to Tucson, I can't stop thinking about him. Not that I ever have. Jackson Arden had been on my mind in one way or another since I was fifteen, and it looks like that's never going to change.

I don't lie to myself about my reasons. Part of me wants to be in Jackson's life, wants us to hook up again, and I can't deny that. Maybe that's why I gave in to him in Albuquerque that first night—or maybe it was the fact that I've always wanted Jackson and he had only given me the time of day once, when I was seventeen, and I was starved for more. It had been stupid to even *go* to the concert, but when I saw an advertisement online about Jack and the Spades, I'd had to go.

The band had been in the early stages when I had last spoken to Gemma, and I'm proud of Jackson for bringing them so far. They were popular around the Midwest, now, and making good money. I always knew that Jackson would go places, but I hadn't imagined it would happen this quickly.

Gemma says they are working on a new album now, and my heart swells with pride for him, even if we barely know each other now. I don't deny that I still love him just as much as I did as a teenager. I just don't want him to know it.

"You're married now?" Gemma asks, and I scoff.

"The father ran off the second I told him I was pregnant," I explain, telling her the words I have been telling everyone.

Gemma sighs. "I'm so sorry, Su-Zoe."

"You're getting better at that already." I grin, and Gemma laughs, loud and open. I think I've missed her just as much as I've missed Jackson. Having a best friend would have helped wonders while I was pregnant with Elijah, but I'm glad I have her now.

Luckily, as a stylist, I'll be working with Gemma more than the guys. She makes it clear that she runs the show as their manager, and all I have to do is get their measurements and find some real rocker outfits for them.

"What are you thinking for the Tucson show?" Gemma asks, and I tilt my head, thinking.

"Leather. Leather pants, white T-shirts, leather jackets. Some of them can be graphic tees, if the guys want."

"I don't care what they want," Gemma jokes, although I'm not one hundred percent sure she's joking. "Whatever you decide for tomorrow night is what they'll wear."

I nod, trying to think of how I'm going to work my tiny budget into clothes for four guys.

Gemma rummages around in her purse on the floor and then stands up, handing me a credit card.

"Here's the business card. Try to keep it under five thousand for the first show, if you can," she says easily, and I gape at her, surprised.

"You guys really *are* doing well," I comment, and Gemma shrugs.

"We are, but I'm just frugal with money. I'm working on buying us a used tour van so we don't have the expense and deposit of renting it, and that'll save us a lot."

Gemma always was mature beyond her years, different than me. I'd always kind of flown by the seat of my pants, just going where the wind blew me and pursuing whatever passion I had at the time. For a few years, it had been designing clothes. Before that, it had been Jackson. Now, I need to reconcile the two of them. At least I won't be working with him closely.

"Do you still sing?" Gemma asks, and I frown a little, confused.

"I mean, not professionally. I kill it at karaoke, though."

Gemma giggles. "Well, do you think you could do a few lines as a backup on the album?"

I try not to visibly react. "Aw, Gemma, I'm a stylist, not a singer," I complain, and she sighs.

"I know, Jackson's just been really struggling with the last couple of songs, not having anyone. I was hoping I didn't have to hire someone else."

I think about some girl working closely with Jackson in

the studio, putting her hand on his bicep as they work, and I wrinkle my nose involuntarily.

"I'll give it a try, if you don't fire me after this first style," I joke.

What the hell am I doing? This is a bad idea. I shouldn't work so closely with Jackson, not after the way we were on the tour. It's only a few lines, though, right? I certainly don't want any other girl doing it, so I have no choice.

Jackson may not be mine, but I'll be damned if I let another girl slide in on him while I'm around.

Chapter 3

Jackson

Gemma comes into the studio like a whirlwind, brandishing a bunch of clothes over one arm.

"I need you to try these on," she says, as if I'm not sitting at the laptop working on melodies.

"I'm a little busy, Gem," I say, and Gemma huffs.

"Well, take a break. I already hired a backup singer for you, anyway. She'll be here in ten minutes."

I glare at her. "You hired someone without my permission?"

Gemma rolls her eyes. "It's *Zoe*. She's a great singer, and she's cheap."

Fuck. My sister is inviting the girl I had a fling with on tour, her best friend from high school, into my studio to work closely with me.

On second thought, that isn't such a bad idea. Zoe does have a wonderful voice, and I can be alone with her this way, ask her why the hell she hadn't told me who she was.

"Shouldn't say such things about your best friend," I crack, and Gemma groans.

"Don't be a jerk, Jackson. What have you got against

15

Zoe, anyway? You ran out of there like the garage was on fire yesterday."

"Nothing," I insist. "I just don't remember her much, that's all."

That much was true. The blue-haired beauty that I'd met in Albuquerque was far from the mousy girl that I'd barely been around while Gemma was in high school. She might have had a crush on me, but I'd barely known her, after all.

I know Zoe more from just a fling on tour than the whole time we spent together when she was a teen, which wasn't very much.

"Well, be nice. She's helping you out as a favor to me," Gemma says, and my jaw tightens.

Of course she is. Because God forbid she want to be alone with me after rejecting me back in Albuquerque. I'm pissed off about it, if I'm honest with myself. It's like she wants to pretend that none of that ever happened, that it's some dirty little secret since she's friends with Gemma.

I wanted to really build something with her, and she just turned me down flat. It felt like a betrayal that she didn't tell me who she really was, either, that she was my little sister's best friend. That seems like lying, and I hate to be lied to. It's one of the worst things I can think of in a relationship. My parents used to lie to us all the time to make up for their lack of parenting skills, or for the lack of food or a clean house or anything, really.

"Try these on," Gemma says and scurries out the door with the rest of the clothes, presumably to take to Axel, Locke, and Samuel, who were working in the room next to me on a melody for a new song. I'd join them soon, but for now, I need the peace and quiet to finish some stuff.

When Locke and then Axel decided to take several

weeks off for paternity leave, I was left with nothing much to do, so I decided to write music instead.

The music I have been writing lately can take the Spades into a different direction and there are a few songs I'm working on that will require a female voice along with mine. It won't work with any of the guys' voices. But it needs to be the right voice. So, I'm surprised that Gemma hired Zoe, but I guess since she's already on the payroll, it's cheaper than hiring someone else.

Zoe shows up in half an hour and knocks quietly on the door despite the door being unlocked. I stand with a sigh and open it, standing in the doorway.

"Hey, stranger," I drawl, and she flushes prettily. She's so petite even though she's got dangerous curves. She's wearing a blouse and a denim skirt, and the sight of all that skin is already making my mouth water.

"Hey," she says quietly, sneaking under my arm to come into the studio. "So, what are we working on?"

I shut the door, turning to her and leaning back against it, crossing my arms.

"Straight to business, huh? You don't want to tell me why you didn't tell me who you were?"

Zoe scoffs, looking up at me with bright blue eyes. "As if you would have remembered."

I bristle at that, although I guess that she's right.

I hum. "I guess I should have, since you had such a crush on me."

Zoe pales. She's already pretty pale, her skin like porcelain, but she's practically glowing like a nightlight in the dark studio, now.

"Who says I had a crush on you?"

I reach behind me to close the blinds in the studio and

lock the door. "Gemma told me she suspected as much," I say simply.

Zoe backs up toward the table holding my laptop, her ass hitting it as I advance toward her.

"What are you doing?"

"Showing you that I remember you," I murmur low in the back of my throat, sliding my hands up her thick thighs, under the denim.

Zoe keeps eye contact with me, and I stop, waiting for her to push me away. She doesn't.

"You wanted me all the way back then, when you were just a mousy little kid?" I ask, and she turns her face away.

"I wasn't a little kid," she insists, and I chuckle.

"You certainly aren't now. You're all grown up."

I take her chin in my hand, forcing her to look at me as my other hand slides further up her skirt, resting on her hip.

"Jackson," she breathes, and I love the way my name sounds on her lips, love the way she moans into my mouth when I lean down to kiss her. I stick my tongue between her lips and she meets it with her own before sucking on mine, making me gasp and roll my hips against her thigh.

I'm hard as diamond already. This is what she does to me. She'd driven me crazy all tour, flirting with me in those little skirts in the crowd at concerts, and she isn't any different now, showing up with all this skin showing.

"I think you wore this skirt just for me," I murmur, dipping my head to her throat to kiss her there, open-mouthed. "I think you wore it just to drive me crazy."

"I didn't wear it for you," she says stubbornly, but she spreads her thighs when I slip my hand between her legs.

I tease her through her panties, and she covers her mouth with one hand.

I pull it away, my fingers circling her wrist.

"It's soundproofed in here, baby, don't worry," I tell her.

"You're sure?" she asks, and I'm angry all over again, suddenly, sliding my hand underneath her panties.

"Why? You ashamed?" I ask, but she doesn't answer, panting and rolling her hips against my hand.

I slip my fingers around her clit, and she cries out, digging her nails into my shoulders before I curl two fingers inside her, hooking them up just like I know she likes.

"Fuck, *Jackson*," she says again, and I groan.

"Want to fuck you in this studio, bend you over my desk," I pant, and just as she begins to clench around my fingers, there's a sharp rap at the door.

Zoe pushes me away, stepping away from the desk and adjusting her panties, and I'm slower to react, slowly taking my fingers and popping them into my mouth and sucking.

I grin at her as she flushes and frowns. I go to the door, calmly opening it.

"Yes, Gemma?" I just knew it was my little sister, coming to butt in, and I am right.

"I forgot to give you your jacket," she says, shoving a red leather jacket into my arms. I don't know if it's real leather, but the fabric feels nice.

"Thanks," I mutter, and she leans up on her tiptoes to look over my shoulder at Zoe. I turn around and Zoe is smiling at her weakly.

"You can get his inseam for the leather pants now," Gemma says, and I smirk at Zoe before I frown.

"Wait, leather pants?"

Zoe raises her chin. "Leather's in right now, Jackson, or at least faux leather."

"I don't care what's *in*. Leather's uncomfortable as hell!" I complain.

19

"Guess you'll have to get over it," Gemma says with a smile and shuts the door.

"You got a problem with me being your stylist?" Zoe asks, her blue eyes flashing.

"I got a problem with wearing leather," I grumble. "It's hot and sweaty and we'll be on stage for two hours.

"I've got powder for that," she says, and I blink at her.

"*Powder*? Like... baby powder?"

"Kind of," she flushes. She's cute when she gets all flustered.

"You want to 'measure my inseam' now?" I ask teasingly, knowing what that entails since I've had slacks tailored before.

Zoe rifles through her purse and slips out a measuring tape, kneeling down in front of me.

I lick my lips and she looks up at me with a sly grin. "Be still, or I'll end up getting the sizing wrong."

"I like the way you look on your knees," I murmur, and Zoe's blue eyes dart up to look at mine.

"Behave, Jackson," she scolds and shifts to measure my inseam, her fingers just lightly brushing across the hardness in my jeans.

I gasp and want to put my hand into her hair but that seems like too much. I grit my teeth.

"It's a good thing we didn't do this when Gemma was here," I say, and Zoe laughs, the sound melodic to my ears.

"I wouldn't do it like this with Gemma around," she says, cupping me in one hand while measuring with the other.

I choke on air. "I haven't ever had a tailor do *that*."

"Oops, sorry. I'm not a tailor either, just a designer, so maybe I'm rusty." She grips me tighter, and I thrust forward into her hand out of instinct.

"You don't like it when you're on the other end of the teasing?" she asks, and I groan as she runs her fingers along my erection.

"I didn't say I didn't like it."

"Hmm," Zoe murmurs. "I bet you'd like my mouth on you more."

"Oh, God, yes, *please*," I beg, but Zoe just giggles and finishes my inseam on both sides, driving me crazy with her hands all over my thighs and erection.

I'm panting by the time she stands up, and all I want to do is bend her over the studio couch, but her blue eyes are twinkling at me mischievously.

"Gotta go," she says simply, and I whine.

"You can't go. Not now," I complain.

"Have to pick up the kiddo," she says, and I grumble and adjust myself in my pants, still uncomfortably aroused, but I can't argue with that, I like Elijah and I know from what Zoe's told me that he gets nervous when his mom is late picking him up. I wouldn't want him to get panicky. I don't like thinking about anything bad happening to Elijah *or* Zoe. I haven't felt this way about anyone in a long time, and with her back in town, maybe it is time to get past my bitterness from her not telling me that she was Gemma's friend and ask her...

Before I can finish my train of thought she's walked out the door, shutting it quietly behind her.

Damnit. Gemma always told me my brain moves too slow, but this is ridiculous.

Chapter 4

Zoe

After what happened with Jackson in the studio, I know that I have to get the hell out of there. There's still an hour before I have to pick up Elijah, but Jackson doesn't know that. I've been playing with fire ever since I first met him in Albuquerque on tour, but now the fire was getting hotter and hotter. It's almost like I'm dumping gasoline on it, really.

I can't keep being stupid about Jackson Arden, or my whole life is going to blow up. I shouldn't have even taken this job, but here I am, planning my next day to measure all the guys. I could probably have eyeballed Jackson's measurements, since I've seen all of him and remembered his body viscerally, but the same can't be said for the rest of the members. Locke wasn't even around when I left town.

Elijah is quiet on the way home, which is unusual. He's as loud and outgoing as his father.

"Everything okay, honey?" I ask, looking at him through the rearview mirror.

He frowns, his little cheeks puffing out. "Where's my daddy?"

22

All the oxygen seems to go out of the room, I had known this time would come, but I hadn't expected it to come before he even started school. Elijah goes to a daycare nearby and he's preparing for pre-school.

"What do you mean?"

"Sarah's daddy comes to pick her up from daycare. Every day. Louie's daddy came to pick him up today. My daddy never comes to pick me up. Why is that?"

There's curiosity in his voice, but not fear or sadness, and for that much, I'm grateful. I guess he doesn't know to miss his father if he's never had one.

"Your daddy isn't around anymore, Elijah," I say dumbly, not knowing what else to say. I don't want to outwardly lie to him, but he's four, surely he won't look too far into it.

"Is he dead? Like Sarah's grandpa?"

Damnit. I know my kid is smart, but I wasn't expecting this. "No, he's not, honey, he's just... not around."

"So, he's lost?" Elijah asks.

That's close enough, I suppose.

"Yeah, he's lost," I say simply, turning into the driveway of my little apartment. It's not much, only a one-bedroom, but it will do until I start making money with Gemma and The Spades. Elijah deserves his own room.

"He'll come home," Elijah says confidently, and my chest aches.

"Maybe," I say dismissively, and change the subject. "Want to watch Paw Patrol?"

"Rescue Bots!" he screeches, and I inwardly groan. There are kid's shows I can stand and kid's shows that I can't stand, and Rescue Bots isn't my favorite. I make a meal I know Elijah will eat, just boxed macaroni and cheese, and sit down on the couch with him to watch.

This is my life, alone at home with my little guy, eating macaroni and cheese and watching Rescue Bots. Just me and Elijah, with his missing dad. His *lost* dad.

Guilt feels hot at the back of my head, because I know exactly where his father is. I bring Elijah closer to me, one arm around his little body, and he snuggles up next to him.

I doze off halfway through the second episode. When my macaroni slides off my plate and our little dog, Scout, comes to scarf it up, I wake up with a start and there is only one thought on my mind.

Tomorrow, I can avoid Jackson. That's why I got his measurements first, after all. I don't have to see him at all.

* * *

The first person I see when I walk into Gemma's house is Jackson. I avert my eyes from him as he smiles at me slyly. Gemma, on the phone with someone, doesn't seem to notice.

"Axel, if you don't get your ass down here *right now*," she snaps.

Samuel smiles at me, sitting down on Gemma's couch, and Locke has baby Cain cradled in his arms, cooing at him.

I stare at Locke, shocked. At his public appearances, he doesn't come across as a talkative person and I don't think I've ever seen him smile on purpose, but he is talking up a storm to this little baby, grinning at him and bouncing him up and down. I guess kids change people, but when he gives Gemma a fond look, I think Gemma might have changed him just as much as Cain did.

"You should have brought yours," Gemma whines when she hangs up the phone. "I think Axel might have to bring over Jazz after all, Harley's sick. We could have had a trio."

"Elijah would love all these babies," I confess. "But I just didn't want him getting in the way. Your babies can't walk yet, so they aren't the demons they will be when they can."

Gemma laughs. "I guess you're right. Cain's starting to roll around and he already wants to get into everything."

"Well, luckily, there's not a whole lot to do today. I just need to take measurements for the leather pants and jackets."

Jackson pales. "You have to do the measurements on *all* the guys?"

I tilt my head. "Well, of course I do. Everyone's measurements are gonna be different." I nod my head toward Samuel and Locke. "Sam and Locke are tall, so they'll have longer pants than you and Axel. Axel's wide, so his leather jacket will be a bit wider across the shoulders."

Jackson bristles and I can tell that he doesn't like the way I'm talking about the guys. I hide a grin. I can't deny that it makes me feel giddy to see him so jealous. I know it's an old, outdated, and totally wrong kind of thing, but jealousy makes me feel that he wants me, and he doesn't want anyone else to have me.

I can't help finding that arousing.

"Let's do your inseam first," I tell Samuel, sticking out my hand to help him up from the couch, and he takes it, smiling at me.

Jackson's gritting his teeth in the corner as I carefully measure Samuel's inseams. Samuel himself is blushing a bright pink, which is cute as a button. He's not my type, but he's adorable nonetheless. I guess I've always been attracted to older men–like Jackson.

Gemma gives me a sideways look but she doesn't say anything, and I figure the worst that might happen is she accuses me of having a crush on the youngest band member. I don't mind if she thinks that, as long as she doesn't put it together that Jackson is the member I have the crush on.

She might just put two and two together in a way that I know Jackson won't. He hadn't even remembered me from when we were kids, after all. Does he even remember the night we hooked up? I don't think he does, or else he would have mentioned it at some point when we were hooking up on tour.

I still can't believe I followed him to three different cities like a groupie, leaving Elijah with my mother after leaving Albuquerque. Elijah loves spending time with his grandmother, so it wasn't bad for him or anything, but it was bad for *me*.

I've spent my whole life trying to get over Jackson Arden, and now here I am, working for him indirectly. I know that this could all blow up, but I think that I can navigate it just right so that I can save money to get my own place, and then get the hell out of here. I can quit as soon as the big tour is over. It'll be seasonal work, anyway, the guys don't tour during the summer months. It's too hot and not as many people go out. It'll be a little tough to get childcare for Elijah but his daycare does overnight visits and my mother or my sister can keep him when I have to end up flying to the next city.

This is just temporary. I need this job, because Elijah's getting bigger and he needs his own space. I'm tired of having Paw Patrol sheets on my bed and having a little guy kicking me in the ribs just like he did when he was in the womb. I just need to work this tour, just six weeks, and then I'll get a big bonus at the end like Gemma promised.

I take my time with Samuel, but I'm done in just a few moments with Jackson staring at me. Well, glaring might be a better term, his green eyes so much like my son's that it's almost eerie. Elijah's are not only the exact same color as Jackson's but they are shaped just like his, too, wide and with long-lashes. They haunt me every day of my life.

Gemma has the same eyes, and although I never met their parents, I think it must run in the Arden genes.

I pat Samuel's shoulder. "Okay, now for the back and shoulders while we wait for Axel."

Jackson opens his mouth and then closes it again when Gemma speaks.

"I'm going to skin him alive if he doesn't bring that baby girl," Gemma seethes, and just then, Axel burst through the door, holding said baby girl in a carrier with one hand.

"Jazzie!" Gemma coos, and Locke smiles a little as if in spite of himself. Locke certainly seems like the possessive type, and Axel's always been a flirt. I'd had to leave town not long after The Spades banded together, pre-Locke, but I remember Axel being flirty with all the fans even back then.

Axel smiles brightly, and I'm struck for a moment how boyish he looks. Axel can be a little intimidating since he's so wide and muscular, but now that his hair has started to grow out a little and he's holding a baby carrier, he looks brighter, younger somehow.

"You remember Susie, right, Ax?" Gemma asks, and Axel looks over at me with a raised eyebrow.

"This is little Susie? Wow, you sure grew up!" Axel says brightly, and Jackson glares at him instead of me this time.

"It's Zoe, now," I say, unable to help smiling back. His bright white toothy smile is contagious, and it's only a bonus that it seems to rankle Jackson when I'm friendly with the members.

"Zoe. Rock on."

Gemma is already taking the baby carrier from him,

unbuckling the snoozing, bald little girl with a bow on her head.

"She's gonna grow out all that blonde hair any day now," Axel says jokingly. "I swear she's not gonna look like my dad forever."

Gemma frowns at him. "She's *beautiful*, Axel, don't you dare."

"She is," he agrees. "Where's my handsome boy?"

"*My* handsome boy is with his Daddy," Locke grumbles, but there's nothing bitter behind it. He smiles a little as Cain squeals at Axel.

It's nice, seeing them all like this. I like knowing that Jackson has a family, someone to back him up. God knows he'd needed it when we first met.

The first time I met Jackson, I saw the pain behind his eyes, and I wanted to know what it was, wanted to take it from him. But after what had happened the last time we were together, I ran from it, as soon as I could. I had loved him so much, and the way he had acted... I can't think about that right now, though, or I'll get into a spiral, so I focus on the baby girl that Gemma is cooing at.

"Isn't she *gorgeous*?" Gemma asks. "Almost makes me want another one."

"Not yet," Locke groans. "We can't have a newborn while we're on tour, and we need to do a couple of them to keep our fans happy."

"I know, I *know*," Gemma mumbles. "I'm just saying, as soon as Jack and the Spades makes it really big, then I'm going to have *all* the babies."

I wrinkle my nose. "I think I'm one and done. Don't think I could do that again. I love my kiddo but being pregnant was the pits."

"Harley thinks so, too," Axel pipes up, sitting down next

to Locke and making faces at the baby. "Gemma's the only crazy one."

Gemma pouts. "After the first few months, it wasn't so bad. I thought it was cool having something kicking around inside me."

"God, Elijah kicked so *hard*," I groan.

Gemma laughs. "I guess if Cain was heavy footed, I wouldn't be so eager to do it again, either."

"I'm clearly Jazz's favorite," Jackson says, moving forward to take the baby, and she falls asleep against his shoulder as he hums to her.

My heart aches, watching him with that baby, knowing he's never gotten to do that with Elijah. And my baby never had that. No dad to carry him or play with him. It was always just me. And yes, it had been my choice, but it still hurts. I feel guilty about it sometimes, but Jackson had been such a mess back then, and I'd been so young...And I'd definitely done the right thing because it would have meant that I would have ruined his life.

I tap Samuel's thigh to get him to stand up and he does, obliging me easily. I stretch the measuring tape across his back, taking my time, trailing my fingers along his back and shoulders, and there's a muscle jumping around in Jackson's jaw as he stares at me.

I look Jackson right in the eyes and then whistle, looking back at Samuel. "Twenty-four inches. That's almost two feet!"

Axel whoops and Gemma shushes him, since Locke has just gotten Cain to sleep.

"Go, Samuel," Axel says more quietly, grinning, and then stands up so that I can measure his inseam. I do take a little extra time because Axel is wider and shorter than the others that I'd measured, but it's nothing like what I did with Samuel just to piss Jackson off.

Jackson huffs nonetheless, and he looks up at me after putting the baby down on the couch, putting pillows around her so that she won't fall.

"Isn't it my turn, now?"

"I already know your measurements pretty well," I say simply, and Jackson makes a face.

"No, you don't. I've grown since you had that big crush on me in high school," he insists, and I gape at him.

"Shots fired," Axel giggles, and I glare at him. He shuts up but he's still laughing, and even Samuel is smiling.

Traitors.

"I regret ever telling you that," Gemma says, and I groan.

"Thanks for that," I grumble, but I measure Jackson's shoulders all the same, slightly less wide than Samuel and Axel, but barely. Jackson has always been tall and lanky, after all, although he was muscular with a six pack, which I knew intimately.

I would only have to tailor Locke's pants because they are a little too short, and Samuel's jacket, because I'd underestimated how wide his shoulders were.

I tell Gemma as much and she grins.

"You're saving us money already. You have no idea the amount of clothes we've had to return because of Locke's long legs and Samuel's wide shoulders. Then there was that one time Axel's bicep ripped out a seam on stage."

Axel kisses his bicep dramatically and I laugh. Jackson's still frowning at me.

"Everything should fit you perfectly," I told Jackson. "I told you that I knew your measurements."

"You really *did* have a crush on him in high school," Axel marvels, and I want to hit him but I refrain.

"I'm a fashion person. I size everyone up the first time I see them," I insist, and that much is true. For example, Gemma's put on some weight since high school and the baby that looks good on her. Not that I'd ever tell her that, unless she asked, of course. She's gorgeous both ways.

I look down at myself, wishing I had Gemma's figure. I'm hippy, pear-shaped, and although men never seem to mind, sometimes I worry that I'm too heavy. Being in the world of fashion as a curvier woman can be difficult, but I try to navigate it with grace.

Styling Jack and the Spades would be a big job for me, and it would get me the deposit and first month's rent for the new two-bedroom apartment I was angling for, so I just have to get through this twelve-week tour, and then things will be okay. I can disappear again, stay away from Jackson and Gemma so that I don't worry about either of them finding out.

"You want to follow me to the studio?" Jackson asks, jerking his head toward the door. "We've got some background tracks to lie down."

I flush, unsure. "I don't know, I need to pick up Elijah from the sitter."

"It'll only take an hour," Jackson insists, and I find myself getting in my car and following him to the studio.

Of course, I still can't say no to Jackson Arden.

Chapter 5

Jackson

Zoe Carmicheal, formerly Susie Carmicheal, my little sister's once and present best friend, is driving me fucking *crazy*.

Who shows up to a fitting in a pair of yoga pants stretched so tightly across her ass that I can see every curve? Zoe does, apparently. I don't like the way she flirted with Samuel, either. Not one bit.

I'll admit it. I'm a possessive guy. I've had my struggles with jealousy in nearly every relationship I've ever been in, but this time, it's different. I feel less secure, less confident, because we haven't actually been out on a date yet. Not for my lack of trying, but Zoe was squirrelly. We just have a casual relationship, and I'm not sure how to quite navigate my jealousy. Do I tell her that I'm jealous? Do I demand that she stop flirting with my friends? Somehow, I don't think that would go over well.

It comes out of my mouth anyway, the second she shuts the studio door. I sit down at the desk and she's standing, biting at her cuticles.

"What the hell do you think you were doing, flirting

with Samuel like that?" I ask, my voice sounding clipped and even, instead of raising in volume. Honestly, I'm not sure she was flirting, at least not on purpose.

Zoe smirks at me and it just makes my blood boil hotter.

"Why do you care?"

"He's too young for you," I growl.

Zoe raises a dark, well-groomed eyebrow.

"Does that mean you're too old for me, Jack?"

I groan. "I'm not old. You're just young. You're my sister's best friend, for God's sake."

"And you've got a problem with that?" Zoe saunters toward me, her hips and ass swaying, making my tongue dart out to wet my dry lips. *Fuck.* I want to grab onto those hips, pull her close, press my face into the cleft of her sex.

Instead, I draw in a deep breath through my nostrils.

"No. I have a problem with you flirting with my band mates," I burst out. Stupid. Now she holds all the cards.

Zoe grins. "Jackson, are you *jealous*?"

"Hell yes, I'm jealous," I grunt. "What do you think? I've been chasing you around for *weeks* but you give Samuel attention the first time you see him in years?"

"Poor baby," Zoe croons. "You want my attention?"

"All of it," I admit, eyeing her hips and thick thighs, and she straddles my lap and my hands instantly go to her ass, bouncing her against me and groaning.

"All you had to do was ask," she whispers in my ear, nipping at my earlobe, and God, I'm going to fuck her right here, rip these yoga pants down and–

Zoe stands up and I pout at her.

"What are you doing? Where are you going?" I whine.

"You said we had to lay down some background tracks. I really *do* have to pick up my kid, you know?"

"You could bring him here," I suggest, and she snorts.

"Not with you unable to keep your hands off me."

"I can never keep my hands off you," I agree, and she laughs, covering her mouth with her hand in a gesture I'd noticed a lot. It's cute. *She's* cute, and now she's off-limits, and that makes me want her even more.

I can imagine the hell that Gemma would give me if she found out I was fucking her best friend. *Especially* since I'd had such an attitude about her dating Locke.

"You haven't asked about taking me out since we met back up," she says slowly. "Does that mean you don't want to anymore?"

"No," I insist, but then I sigh. "But it's probably not a good idea, given you're Gemma's best friend and all." I point at her. "Which you *lied* to me about."

"I didn't lie," she protests. "I just didn't tell you who I was. You should have remembered me, you know?"

"I was a mess the last time we met," I say. "I'm sorry I didn't recognize you, but I do now."

A mess is probably an understatement. Back then, With all the shit with my parents and having to take care of Gemma, I was way over my head and drowning. I hadn't been good enough for anyone back then, and sometimes, I wonder if I'm good enough now. I went through some rough times and I know Gemma and the guys had to pull me out of a dark hole, but I've changed, and I want to show Zoe that I'm different now.

"Is it weird?" she asks. "Seeing me all grown up?"

I lick my lips again. "Super weird. But it's kind of hot, too." I groan. "I hate myself, but even when you were a kid, you were kind of my type."

"Is that so?" Zoe says, as if she's not very surprised, and I frown.

Before I can ask her more questions, she puts on a pair

of headphones and starts harmonizing into the microphone. I quickly turn on the recording equipment and Zoe has nearly a pitch-perfect tone, so it doesn't take long for the background tracks to be laid. I'll sing over them later, after the concert.

"That was fast," I frown, and Zoe smiles.

"Told you I could get it done. I've got to go pick up the kiddo."

"Tell him I said hi," I say idly, and she freezes for a moment before walking out.

When I think about it, Zoe's always been kind of weird about her kid. I'd met him by accident, and she seems not to want me around him. I guess it makes sense, if you're not in a serious relationship, to keep it from your kid. She wouldn't want him getting attached or anything.

Even though I think I'm already attached. To her and to the kid. I know that I fall in love easily, but this is ridiculous. Maybe it's moving faster in my heart because I knew her from before and we'd reconnected, but I had *barely* known her, so this doesn't make a lot of sense to me.

All I know is that I think about her all the time. Hell, I even *dream* about her.

* * *

In my dreams, my vision is doubling, like I've downed a half dozen drinks, but I'd know Zoe's cute button nose and dangerous curves anywhere.

She has long, dark hair instead of the blue bob I've seen her with at the concert.

She is biting at her cuticles, lying down on my bed, and I take her ankles in my hands, yank her to the edge of the bed.

35

"Are you ready, Susie?" I ask her, and she opens her mouth...

And that's when the sound of an alarm comes out of her mouth.

I sit bolt upright, sweating, my dick hard in my boxer briefs and standing up against my belly. *Shit.* What was that? I don't have a teenage fetish, quite the opposite, really. I usually think that older women are more my type, but Zoe is an outlier.

I make my way to the shower, groaning as the water hits my erection, and I know that I'll have to recall the dream to get it out of my system. I run my hands down my body, teasing myself, but that doesn't last long.

I can't get Zoe's piercing blue eyes out of my head, so blue they were almost silver in the moonlight streaming through my window. *Man,* that had been a realistic dream. It was just like my bedroom in the house that Gemma and I had grown up in. My hair had been extra-long, down to half-way down my back the way it had been before I cut it to my shoulders a few years ago. I still kept it long, swept back in a ponytail, but back then, it had been ridiculous.

That's the way Zoe used to look, too, all that long, dark hair, big blue eyes. She'd been a little thinner then, although I love the way she's filled out.

I stroke myself lightly at first and groan, fisting myself, thrusting into my own hand. I remember Zoe teasing me when she measured my inseam, grabbing me over my slacks. She's such a tease when she wants to be.

I remember the way she straddled my lap, the way her ass feels in my hands, more than two handfuls, and I moan out her name as I spill into the shower drain. I'm breathing hard when I finish. That's fast. Faster than usual. I usually make a production out of self-pleasure, but that dream was something else. Zoe makes me feel like that, ever since we've started hooking up, like I just need to be inside her, need to be filling her up. It's like some pull in my stomach, like it's meant to be or something corny like that.

I hate that I'm still a hopeless romantic, after all these heartbreaks. I sigh and run my hands through my wet hair, washing it and rinsing out the shampoo and conditioner combo my hair stylist hates that I use.

The concert is tonight, and we live about forty-five minutes away from Santa Fe, so I put my clothes in the car, hanging them up to Zoe's specifications. I wonder if she'll be at the concert, wonder if that's part of her job, too, or maybe she'll just come along.

Gemma will give her free tickets, after all, and she's always been a fan of my music, even before I'd started with the Spades. I remember her smiling, singing along to the nineties rock I'd played on my acoustic guitar when we were both younger.

I hope she'll be there. I know it's a bad idea to keep hooking up with Zoe for two reasons: A. she's my little sister's best friend who is working for us. B. I'm falling for her. Fast. Hook, line, and sinker. But I've never been one to make good decisions.

I've always lived life as it comes, and Zoe is just another obstacle–maybe I'll leap over it, and maybe I'll fall flat on my face. Either way, I'm down to see what happens. That's just the kind of guy I am.

Chapter 6

Zoe

I've been telling myself all week that I'm not going to the concert. It's just another opportunity to see Jackson in his element and increase my attraction to him. We're already having issues staying away from each other, and it's barely been a week.

If he'd pushed just a little that day that I'd measured everyone and sat in his lap at the studio, God knows what I would have done.

"Zoe, you *have* to come," Gemma whines when I tell her that I can't.

"I don't have a sitter," I lie. My mother will be more than willing to watch Elijah, but I haven't asked her, thinking that I shouldn't go.

"You can use my sitter," Gemma says, as if she's had a lightbulb go off over her head. "She's keeping both Jazz and Cain, and I bet she'd love to have a little guy to help her."

"Elijah is very helpful," I say hesitantly.

Damnit. I know myself, and I know if Gemma asks one more time...

"Please?" she asks, and I cave.

"Sure. What's one night?"

* * *

Oh my God. Leather pants was such a bad idea. Such a *monumentally* bad idea. Jackson looks so good it's criminal, with all that brown hair in a low ponytail, a white T-shirt that's basically see-through, and a black leather jacket with black leather pants, all perfectly tailored to him. The diamond studs I'd picked out for the guys that have pierced ears shine and look great on him, too.

I'm going to hyperventilate. He's on the stage, looking all the world like a rock god, and I can't believe I've been having sex with this man. How did I get so lucky? What am I *doing* not having sex with him right now?

Calm down, Zoe, I tell myself. He's just a man. He's just Jackson, your best friend's stupid older brother who you've been in love with for seven years and it's not a problem. *It's fine.*

"You did such a good job on the outfits!" Gemma yells over the soundcheck. "I want to eat Locke alive."

"That was the idea," I say wanly, and Gemma grins.

"Let's get a drink. Mama's night out, right? You got a ride home?"

I shake my head and she shrugs, pushing a shot into my hands when she hails the bartender.

"Jackson will take you home. He's on a sobriety streak since the tour. Hopefully, this one will stick."

He'd been drinking on the tour, and I had thought that was why he hadn't remembered me. Now I'm not so sure. Maybe I just... wasn't that memorable.

I took in a deep breath. No reason to think like that, not just yet, anyway. What I needed to do was get all my hormones under control and be serious about not sleeping with Jackson anymore. The more I sleep with him, the closer I get to falling in love, and that's bad. Very bad, considering that I have a child who's four years old with his eyes. A child he doesn't know is his and that I never want him to find out is his.

Keep it together, Zoe. I tell myself when I take a second shot with Gemma, but after the third shot, all bets are off and I want to take off my clothes right there in the mosh pit.

Jackson winks at me after he belts out a particularly spicy line, and I scream, I can't help it. Gemma giggles at me, tipsy and leaning against me and whooping for Locke's drum solo.

I make my way to the bar just before their set is over, and thankfully, it's Samuel who sits next to me while I order a water, ordering a beer.

"Hey, wide shoulders," I say, a little drunk, and Samuel blushes.

He laughs softly.

"You're drunk, Miss Stylist."

"Only a little. Call me Zoe," I insist, and he smiles at me.

"Okay. You're drunk, *Zoe,*" he drawls.

"I don't get out much," I admit, sipping my water. "I'm taking a water break, don't worry."

"Better drink two bottles," a voice behind me says, and I turn around to see Jackson frowning at me. "Did my sister make you take shots of that shitty vodka she likes?"

"It's not shitty," I insist. "Tastes like nothing."

"That's what makes it shitty. Dangerous. Gives you a hell of a hangover. I should know," Jackson warns, ordering himself a bottle of water as I sip mine.

I look up at him from under my eyelashes. "You did great up there."

He grins at me, his frown finally fading. "Thanks. You look good, too," he murmurs, looking me up and down.

I'm proud of my choice in dress, a little club dress that's blue like my eyes and sequined. I think it brings out my curves and it seems like Jackson agrees.

I turn back to Samuel but he's gone, flitted off somewhere, maybe the dance floor. They have a half hour break before they go back to finish the second half of the set.

"Where'd my friend go?" I pout.

"*I'm* your friend," Jackson insists. "I'm your ride home, remember?"

"I remember," I say darkly, and Jackson laughs a little.

"Not your number one choice?" he asks.

"You always are," I mumble, but thank God he doesn't seem to hear me, holding a hand up to his ear as if the music is too loud. "Nothing. Never mind," I yell over the music, and he nods.

He takes my hand as if I'd told him something important, pulling me toward the hallway where the bathrooms are. It's quieter there, and he leans down to whisper in my ear.

"That dress is killing me."

I look up at him, the vodka making me bold. "What are you gonna do about it?"

Jackson growls against my ear, presses me up against the wall in the hallway, and proceeds to suck a mark onto the base of my throat while I writhe and moan beneath him. He has one hand looped loosely around my throat and I wish he'd press harder, press his thumbs into my flesh, mark me that way, too.

I'm the one who leads him into the women's bathroom,

locking the door of the single bathroom, because I'm drunk and horny and well... I'm stupid about Jackson Arden.

"Look at you," he murmurs, bending me over the sink so that I can see my open mouth, the way he's smeared my lipstick by kissing me. I can see my cleavage spilling out of my top, the way Jackson's hands go to my hips as he presses his erection against me.

"Jackson," I gasp. "Hurry."

I'm already so wet that I'm soaking the thong I'm wearing and he curses when he pulls it down to my ankles, working his thigh between my legs to spread me open, bunching my dress up around my hips.

It hasn't been that long since we've hooked up in a club bathroom, but this feels different, more taboo somehow, with his sister outside in the crowd.

"Impatient. Look at you, soaking through your panties," he mumbles. His words are slow from lust instead of alcohol, and I want him so bad I can't stand it.

I roll my hips back, pushing back against him. "I want you inside me, right now, Jackson, please."

"Eager baby," he whispers. "Everyone right outside, if there was a skip in the music, they could hear you beg for me, couldn't they?"

It takes him a long moment to work the leather down his body and free himself, and he rubs against my slick heat before entering me, groaning loudly.

"Could hear how much you like fucking me, too," I gasp as I'm jolted forward by Jackson's hips, his hands all over my ass, grabbing handfuls and watching it jiggle.

"God, I *love* fucking you," he admits, his hips moving faster. "I've been wanting to do it all night, the whole time I was playing. I was singing to you, you know that?"

Fuck. I always imagine that Jackson's singing to me, I've

done it since I was young, and to know that it's really happening feels very surreal.

"Faster, harder," I breathe, my breath fogging up the mirror and I can see my makeup running from sweat. I'm going to have to do some cleanup before I leave this bathroom, but I don't care. I can still remember the first club we hooked up in, not in Albuquerque but in Dallas, and he'd thrown me up against the stall door, fucked me standing up.

This is better, I think. I like feeling him behind me, like having his hands on my hips so he can snap me back toward him, angle deeper inside me. He starts to hit a sweet spot a few moments in and I begin to come all over him, crying out and grabbing hold of the sink so hard it's a wonder it doesn't break off in my hands.

"Oh my God," Jackson pants. "I'm so close. You're so fucking hot and slick, Zoe, so wet for me. Tell me it's for me, yeah?"

He sounds desperate, like that's what he needs to tip over the edge, and I'm no stranger to his possessive dirty talk, after all. Jackson likes what he likes, and he's always been like this.

"All for you, baby," I manage before I gasp when he spills inside of me, groaning and grabbing so tight on my hips I know I'll have thumbprint bruises.

My legs are shaking when he pulls out of me, looking down at his watch, the one I picked out for him earlier that week.

Jackson smirks at me, slapping me on the ass. "Let's do that again tonight," he whispers in my ear, and I shudder all over.

Am I going to do it? I look at myself in the mirror, trying to fix my makeup, washing my face and patting the sweat in my cleavage. This is maybe the sluttiest thing I've ever done, letting Jackson fuck me over a dirty club sink, but even when I think about it, I'm not sorry.

I don't think I'll be sorry if I leave Elijah overnight and spend the night with Jackson, either.

What the hell am I thinking? I can't do this!

I exit the bathroom, telling myself under no circumstances will I stay the night with Jackson Arden.

Chapter 7

Jackson

My sister really does a number on the vodka and Zoe, because I basically have to carry her out of there.

She's hanging all over Samuel's arm, even though that's probably only because she can barely stand up, and he's tipsy and giggly, and I *hate* it, so I just walk over to her and pick her up, throwing her over my shoulder.

Her head hangs down and she squeaks a little, but she doesn't stop me, giggling as we enter the parking garage. We've all brought our own cars to Santa Fe since we have a week break before driving out to Dallas, and I'm grateful that I did, given the state that Zoe is in.

"Are we going home?" Zoe asks when I buckle her in, looking at me with glassy blue eyes, and I shake my head.

"Not home. My hotel room."

"I don't have a hotel room," she mumbles. "Was gonna go home."

"You're not driving home in this state," I say dryly. "So, you're coming with me."

Zoe crosses her arms over her chest. "I'm not sleeping with you."

I laugh. "I wouldn't try, not with you like this. You're about two shots past consent."

She tears up, sniffling. "You don't want to sleep with me?"

I roll my eyes and roll the window down slightly, knowing from my own drunken experiences that fresh air feels better than the air conditioner.

"Of course I want to sleep with you. How about this, when we get there, you drink some water, and I'll let you sleep in my bed."

"Can we cuddle?" she asks brokenly, and she's so cute I want to kiss her right then and there.

"Yeah, yeah, of course. I'm a cuddle master, right?"

"You do have good cuddle arms," she slurs, poking my bicep. "You're strong. Picked me right up."

"You're light as a feather," I tell her.

She grins at me. "You make me feel that way. Always throw me around." She looks at me from underneath her eyelashes again. "Are you sure we can't have sex?"

"Pretty sure you'd fall asleep halfway through," I laugh, and she laughs back, seeming less upset.

"Yeah, probably. You were right about the vodka. It's dangerous."

You're dangerous, I want to say. *Dangerous because you're sitting in my car, drunk and adorable, and all I want to do is tell you that I've fallen for you.* It is too soon for that. It is too soon for me to be *feeling* that, and besides, I'd told myself I had to keep things casual. The last time I'd fallen too hard and too fast, it nearly killed me. She's my little sister's best friend. She's a single mom. She works with us. It'll be too much drama. Who knew if the baby's father was still in her life? I feel my jaw clench up at the thought. He's probably texting her, begging to get her back every couple of days. I tell myself I'll ask her about it, but not tonight.

Tonight, I'm going to enjoy cute, tipsy Zoe.

I help her out of the car and she leans into me in the elevator, seemingly nearly falling asleep. She's thankfully awake when we get into the hotel room, though, and she hops up on the desk, nearly falling over as I grab her a bottle of water.

"M'hungry," she mumbles. "Should have went to get food."

I pull out my phone. "I'll order us some burgers and fries. How about that?" I ask, and she grins drunkenly up at me.

"You're an angel, Jackson Arden. My own personal angel," she gushes, and I laugh out loud.

"I'm gonna use that when you're sober."

She doesn't seem to mind, kicking her feet and humming in the back of her throat happily.

When the food comes, she all but breaks a leg running to the door, and I grab her around the waist, meeting the delivery guy who I tip extra since my kind of girlfriend almost bowled him over in the hallway.

As Zoe's munching on her fries, she stares at me.

"You really don't remember, do you?"

"Remember what?"

"Me," she says, pouting.

"I remember you," I insist. "It just took me a minute."

"You don't," she insists, wrinkling up her nose.

I put my hand on her thigh. "I'll make up for it, yeah?"

"How are you gonna do that?"

I shrug. "I thought I already did, back in the club bathroom."

"At least twice more, before you're forgiven," she says huffily.

I smile at her. "Twice more in a club bathroom?"

"Twice more, period. Then we should stop," she says firmly.

My heart plummets to my toes. "We should stop? Why?" She's only echoing what I've been thinking for the past few days, but still, I hate the way it makes me feel.

"We're not good for each other. I'm your sister's best friend. I have a baby," she says hesitantly, looking at me as if expecting me to protest.

I nod. "I guess you're right. Two more times, huh? We've got to make them count."

Zoe grins wickedly. "I have some things in mind."

I shake my head. "Not tonight. Tonight I'm going to be a gentleman," I tell her, and she pouts.

"You've never been a gentleman before," she whines, but her eyelids are drooping so I pick her up off the desk and strip off her dress because she keeps complaining about it being hot. I've still got her thong in my pocket so I swallow hard and give her my white t-shirt, which doesn't do much to hide her curvy body. Her nipples peak through the white fabric and I groan, undressing down to my underwear.

"You're not going to make this easy on me, are you?" I ask, and she grins and rocks her hips back against mine while I spoon her.

I bury my face in her neck and bite her there, liking her moan of pleasure. "If you still want to tomorrow, I'm going to rail you into next week," I promise.

Zoe giggles. "I'll always want to," she says sweetly, turning to nuzzle against me and finally my erection starts to go down. She smells like sweat and lavender and she's so soft against me, kissing along my collarbone.

She's snoring lightly long before I can go to sleep, and I think to myself that this is going to be a hell of a difficult web to get myself out of.

I wake up to Zoe scrambling around the hotel room, crawling under the bed to get her dress and I groan.

"It's too early for you to be trying to leave the bed already. It's cold, get your ass back in here."

"I've got to Uber back to my car," she says frantically. "I left Elijah overnight."

"With Simone, right? She's a great sitter, I doubt he even noticed you were gone all night," I say easily. "Cain has the worst separation anxiety but he's fine with her."

"You don't understand," she wails, beginning to cry. "This is the first night I've spent away from him since the tour. He won't understand."

I sit up in bed, frowning. "Did he have a hard time with it when you went on tour with me?"

She had only gone to a couple of different shows in a couple of different cities, and as far as I could remember, only spent the night once.

She shakes her head and sits down on the edge of the bed. "No. I just feel like a horrible mother."

I rub her back, crooning comforts in her ear.

"You're far from a horrible mother. You're a great mom. It's okay to have some adult fun every once in a while," I tell her, and that was something I'd been telling Gemma for months. She agrees with me, though, and it seems like Zoe doesn't.

"It's just weird, you know? Ever since... Well, ever since his father, I haven't done this kind of thing. Not until I saw you again."

I stiffen at the mention of the father. "Where is he, anyway? Does he see Elijah?"

Zoe scoffs. "No. He doesn't even know," she says in a small voice.

Holy shit. What kind of awful person must the father be if Zoe hasn't even *told* him? I hate him even more, now, and I hated him plenty to begin with.

"So, you only feel like a horrible mom because you're doing it alone. All that Elijah has is you," I suggest.

She looks at me, sniffling and wiping at her eyes. "How do you know so much?"

I shrug and grin. "I've dated a lot of single moms."

She hits me in the chest lightly and I laugh.

"That's actually a really astute observation, and you're right. It's okay to have adult fun now and again." she looks me up and down.

"Does that mean you're going to relieve me of my gentlemanly duties?" I ask with a smirk, and she pounces on me, tugging down my boxer briefs and I groan when her fingers wrap around me, as she takes the head of my cock into her mouth and sucks lightly, looking up at me.

I thread my fingers through her bright blue, shoulder-length hair, a little shorter than mine, bobbing her head up and down. She takes me in deeper and I let out a guttural moan that reverberates on the hotel walls. I feel like we're going to get a noise complaint, but I don't care. I'd paid the deposit.

I shudder when she takes me all the way down to my base, using the flat of her tongue to lick along my underside and my tip. It feels so good I feel like I'm close to the edge in just moments, and when she gags around me, I pull her head up, looking her in the eyes.

"Why don't you ride me, baby blue?" I ask her softly,

using the nickname I'd given her because of her blue eyes and even bluer hair.

She's still just wearing my T-shirt, her nipples still hard and poking through the fabric, and I take her breasts in my hands as she straddles me, rubbing herself against my erection.

"I don't think I've ever done this," she says, and my eyes widen.

"With me or anyone?"

"Anyone," she says shyly. "I might not be very good at it."

I thrust up beneath her, unable to control myself. The idea that she's never done this position, that she's inexperienced other than with me, makes me so hot it makes me worry. What does that even say about me as a person? I think it's something to do with how possessive I am, but I don't want to look too far into why I have a sudden innocence kink.

"You're good at everything, baby blue," I tell her, and she sighs, moving her hips forward and taking my underwear all the way out, sliding her wetness across my length.

I grit my teeth as she guides me inside her. She's tight and slick from last night, since we haven't showered. She's still full of me, and that only makes me hotter. I can feel myself pulsing inside her.

"Am I doing okay?" she asks hesitantly, and my hands go to her breasts again, thumbing across those nipples that have been driving me crazy since I put her in my shirt last night. She's full of me, covered in me, and I love it.

"You're doing amazing," I manage, giving little thrusts up beneath her, unable to control them. I want to flip her over and fuck her hard and fast, but this feels so good that I don't want her to stop.

51

She rolls her hips experimentally and I gasp out her name, my hands tightening on her breasts. She moans, moves one of my hands to her throat and I squeeze slightly, knowing from our hookups before that she likes to be choked, likes to be dominated. Even when she's on top, she likes me to be in control, so I thrust up beneath her, rolling my hips to angle up just in the way I know she likes.

"Oh fuck," she moans. "You feel so big like this."

"You feel so tight," I respond, gritting my teeth again, wanting her to have her orgasm before I have mine, but I know it's going to be a near thing since I'm close to bursting.

"Jackson," she breathes. "Jackson, oh Jack."

It sends me over the edge, the way she says my name like that, and I tighten my hand around her throat. As I do, her eyes pop open and she begins to pant, rolling her hips faster and faster. Her orgasm explodes and she clenches around me like a vice, her thighs trembling.

I'm only a few pumps away so I release her throat, take hold of her hips and fuck up into her until I burst, gasping and moaning while she's raking her manicured nails down my chest.

"Jesus fuck," I pant, and she agrees, slowly rolling off me with a groan. "Does that have to count for the first of our two times?"

"I think it *has* to," she says, and she's right, it's too good not to count, her first time on top.

I want to ask her about it, but I'm exhausted from being up late the night before and the sun is just now streaking through the room. She woke up way too early. I snuggle into her, nuzzling her neck and she sighs heavily, sweating and sated.

I'm asleep before my head hits the pillow, instead cradled on her chest.

Chapter 8

Zoe

Well, I did exactly what I said I wasn't going to do. Now here I am, with Jackson's head on my chest and his arms wrapped around me, in his hotel bed.

What happened to *this is the last time*? What happened to *not again, Zoe*? Am I ever going to stop being stupid about Jackson Arden?

It certainly doesn't seem that way, and when I sneak out from under Jackson's arms, he whines and takes the pillow instead, cuddling it to him. I nearly melt into the ground. He's so handsome, so sweet...

Shut up, Zoe, I tell myself. *You can't date him. You know this.*

But why can't I? He doesn't have to know about Elijah. He *never* has to know about Elijah, right? I bite at the cuticle which is already red and bleeding on my thumb. Of course, he'd end up finding out about Elijah. Gemma would figure it out, put it together and tell her brother, and then he'd hate me for lying to him. Not to mention, I still can't trust him. He was such a mess before, drinking all the time, partying, and even if he said he's changed, how can I be sure?

One more time, that's what I said, and now I'm wondering how that's going to be possible given that we work in such close proximity. I have an appointment to record with him in three days, for God's sake. All I can do is get out of here before he wakes.

I manage to find my dress and do the walk of shame downstairs, avoiding Gemma and Locke, who are checking out downstairs.

Gemma catches me as I'm walking outside and I curse inwardly.

"Are you as hungover as I am?" she asks, groaning. "Smart move, getting a hotel room."

Oh thank God. Of course she doesn't automatically think I've spent the night with her brother, that's just my own paranoid brain.

"Yeah," I say easily. "I was pretty lit."

Gemma laughs. "I think I overdid it last night because I really needed a night out with a bestie. I missed that, you know?"

"I know, me too. And it's always good to let loose when you know the kids are safe and taken care of," I tell her, and she smiles at me.

"Yeah, you definitely missed out on your wild years. Maybe I can help with that." she winks at me.

These Ardens are going to be the death of me, I swear. First Jackson and our hooking up with the wildest sex in the wildest places, and now Gemma threatening to get me drunk off that dangerous vodka we'd been shooting last night.

"You riding to your car with Jack?"

"God, no," I burst out. I don't want the final time we have sex to be in the backseat of his car, after all.

"Here, Locke and I will take you back. Jack's probably doing late checkout, anyway. Lazybones," she teases but there doesn't seem to be any bite in it. She loves Jackson, and they've always gotten along, as far as I know.

That might change if she finds out what's been going on, and right under her nose. But that isn't going to happen, because we're only going to do it one more time. Then it will be over and we can both move on.

I get into the backseat and Gemma slides in next to me, putting her head on my shoulder.

"I've been replaced," Locke says dryly, and Gemma hums in agreement.

"I missed my bestie," she murmurs, and my heart seems to swell in my chest.

"I've missed you too, Gem," I say softly, and I mean it. I've missed her terribly, especially through my pregnancy and the worst months when Elijah was a newborn. I wish I had her to talk to, to commiserate with, but I'd pushed her away. All because I didn't want her to know what had happened with her brother, and later I couldn't let her find out that her brother is the father of my child.

I can't help feeling a massive amount of guilt for that, but that's one reason that I can't let Gemma meet Elijah. I know that she'll know right away, my best friend has always been observant, and I just can't risk that. She'll tell Jackson, for sure. Her loyalties will always lie with him, and I understand that.

"How has it been, working with Jackson?" she asks innocently.

"It's been... okay," I say hesitantly.

"He takes that crush thing way too seriously," she

laughs. "How many of us still are crushing on the guy we were crushing on in high school? Honestly."

"Honestly," I echo. I guess I'm a bit of an anomaly there, because the only man I've ever even been with is my high school crush. Don't get me wrong, I'd been on dates, kissed other guys, but I'd never let it get further. I'm always worried about another unexpected pregnancy, and honestly, I've just never felt a spark with anyone else the way that I feel with Jackson. I've never really felt sexually attracted to anyone else. I wish I could tell my best friend all about it, but I can't.

"You didn't have a crush on me when you met me?" Locke asks, pouting, and Gemma snorts.

"You know I couldn't stand you until our last tour," she drawls, and Locke grumbles but there's nothing mean in it. They have a good back and forth, lots of banter, and they seem like a fun couple.

I hope Jackson isn't too upset with me for running out, but honestly, why would he be? We've both decided that it should be casual.

Haven't we?

Three days later, I have the worst morning that I've maybe ever had. Elijah is being a stage-five clinger and begging me not to leave him at daycare, my hair is a dyed mess because I'm trying to touch it up five minutes before I leave, and I've got blue dye all over my hands.

The daycare workers finally manage to pry Elijah off me and I make it to the studio, scrubbing at my hands with antibacterial wipes. The dye isn't coming off and I huff out a breath. Jackson meets me at the studio door.

"You're late," he says coldly.

"Sorry. Elijah was being a holy terror and -" Jackson turns his back on me and I shut my mouth. Clearly, he doesn't care what I have to say or why I'm late.

"I've already recorded my part of this song. I just need you to do the backups over what I've recorded."

I stare at him. "I thought we were supposed to do it together."

"Well, you weren't here, were you?" he snaps.

I put my hands on my hips. "Jackson Arden. Why are you being such an ass all of a sudden?"

"You *left* me," he says firmly, his green eyes shooting to mine where he'd been looking away. "We spent the night together and you just snuck out, like it was a one-night stand."

"Wasn't it?" I ask. "Didn't we say we should stop?"

"That doesn't make it mean nothing, Zoe," he says fiercely, his jaw tight, full lips thinned. "It means *something*,"

I've never imagined Jackson saying something like this to me. It feels like a dream.

"What are you trying to say, Jackson."

He sighs, running a hand across his face. "I'm saying that I *like* you, Zoe. I have... I have feelings for you."

"Don't say that," I mourn, and Jackson smiles softly.

"It's true. I do. It... It hurt my feelings when you left like that," he admits, looking away from me.

I can't help myself. I lean down and take his hands in mine, willing him to look at me. He finally does, biting his lower lip.

"What can I do to make it up to you?" I ask, and his green eyes light up.

"You can let me take you out," he says, and then quickly

continues before I can protest. "A date. A real one. Friday night."

"Jackson—" I start.

"I'll pick you up at seven," he insists.

"I don't have a sitter," I lie, and he scoffs.

"Bring little man with you. He's cool."

I blink at him. "I can't do that, Jackson. I should never have let him..." I trail off, because there's hurt flashing across Jackson's face and that's the last thing I want.

"No excuses, Zoe. Just one date. That's all I ask." He looks up at me, pleading with me, and then slowly, he brings my hands to his mouth, kissing along my knuckles.

Damnit. That does it. How am I supposed to say no *now*?

"Fine. One date, but that counts as sex," I say firmly.

"Only if we have sex on the date," he grins.

I roll my eyes. "We're definitely going to have sex on the date."

Jackson looks me over. "I wish you'd quit dressing like that when you come over here."

I look down at my yoga pants and cut-off T-shirt. It covers me well and I raise an eyebrow.

"What, too casual for you? You want me to wear a dress every time?"

"No," he growls. "I want you to wear something that won't make me want to jump your bones the second you walk in here."

I step away from him, dropping his hands and giggling.

"Can't do that, sorry. I'm too sexy in everything I wear."

"Damn right you are," Jackson agrees and then sighs. "Come over here and plant your ass in this seat. Gemma will skin me if I don't get this done between now and Monday. She's helped pay for the release of this demo."

"I love this song, Blue," I say, blushing a little.

Jackson stares at me. "You should. I wrote it about you."

I gasp. It's a song about feelings, lust too, don't get me wrong, but mostly *feelings*.

"You did not."

"I did. Why do you think I named it Blue?"

He does call me "baby blue" in the softest tone, sometimes. God, this is like a dream come true but I can't enjoy *any* of it for fear that I'll be found out,

"Well then, who did you write Red about?" I ask. That one is definitely a totally different song, one about heartbreak and rage.

Jackson looks away, clearing his throat. "I plead the fifth."

I stare at him curiously. "It's about Maria, isn't it?" I say flatly.

Jackson doesn't answer, but jealousy rolls through me. The song isn't exactly a positive one, more of a hate letter to the girl who broke his heart, but still, if he feels that strongly about it, it still means something to him. She'll always mean something to him, and since no one but Jackson had ever meant anything to me, I don't like it. Not one bit. Especially given that first night we were together.

It's only a two-track mini album, and I'm doing backup singing on both tracks. We focus on Blue today, and Red on Monday. I plan to put my all into *my* song, and maybe half-ass the one about Maria.

I won't do that, but it's really tempting to think about. I do my thing and get about halfway through the song, which takes about half an hour, before there's a banging on the studio door.

Jackson frowns, going to the door, and it's a daycare worker, holding Elijah by the hand.

"I'm so sorry, Ms. Carmichael, but Elijah has a fever, and due to company policy..."

"You can't keep him today," I sigh.

"Exactly. We tried to get in touch with you, but your mother gave us the address to your job–I'm so sorry to have to do this."

Mom must have been at home alone without the car, unable to pick Elijah up, and I'd left my phone on the studio couch.

"I'm sorry," I apologize, taking Elijah's hand. He grabbed me around the waist, turning his head into my stomach. "Thank you for bringing him here."

I turn around to apologize to Jackson as the daycare worker leaves, but he's smiling and crouching down to Elijah's level.

"Not feeling so well, bud?" he asks softly.

Elijah shakes his head. "My tummy hurts," he says quietly.

"You like ginger ale? I keep ginger ale here for when my tummy hurts." Jackson stands up and whispers to me, "Hangovers."

I giggle, putting my hand over my mouth in a gesture I've done my whole life, and Jackson smiles fondly at me before popping a can of ginger ale from the mini-fridge and handing it to Elijah.

Elijah sips it gratefully. "I love ginger ale. Thank you, Mr. Jack."

"How many times do I have to tell you, just call me Jack," Jackson insists. "You wanna listen to some tunes while your mama finishes work?" he asks, and Elijah grins and nods, climbing up onto the couch next to Jackson, who nods at me and flips through his phone to find a song.

I slowly walk into the soundproof studio room, shutting the door behind me, and I sit down in the chair and put on the headphones, watching them through the clear glass. They look so cozy, sitting right next to each other, and as I watch, Jackson crosses his left leg over his right and so does Elijah, in a mirror image. This is exactly what I want. Ever since I was a teenager, I'd wanted me and Jackson together, for us to have a family, and this is what it would look like.

My throat goes dry, and for a moment I wonder if I should get out there and take him home, but instead I close my eyes and finish recording. It takes about an hour, and by the time I turn around again, Elijah is asleep in Jackson's arms and Jackson is smiling at me.

"He fell right asleep listening to The Beatles," he says in awe.

"The *White Album* always puts him right out," I laugh, and Jackson shakes his head.

"He's a hell of a kid," he says.

"Takes after his father," I say, not even thinking about it, and Jackson's eyes dart to mine.

"What is he, a musician?" Jackson accuses, something bitter in his tone.

I shrug. "I have a type, I guess."

"I guess," Jackson grumbles.

I grin at him. "You jealous again?"

Jackson groans. "I'm jealous every time I think about someone else touching you. Drives me crazy," he admits, and I sit next to him.

"Will it help if I tell you no one else has touched me since you started to?" I asked softly, and Jackson's eyes widen.

"Yes. Yes, that would help immensely," he says emphatically, and I giggle.

"Well, it's true. It's been only you since we met up in Albuquerque that night."

"Thank God. Now if you'll stop flirting with Samuel, everything will be perfect," Jackson says, and I laugh again.

"I don't even flirt with Samuel," I scoff, and there's a sharp knock on the door.

"That'll be Gemma," Jackson groans, disentangling himself from my son, and I freeze, panic rising in my throat.

Elijah doesn't just have Jackson's eyes, he has his nose, his jawline–his light brown hair. Gemma will know.

I scoop up Elijah in my arms even as he protests and burst out the door, past Gemma.

"Sorry, sick kid, don't want to infect you and give it to the baby," I burst out in apology, and I get into the car, finally releasing a long breath as I get a grumpy and sleepy four-year-old in the booster seat.

All I can do is hope that this tour goes by faster than I think.

Chapter 9

Jackson

There she goes, leaving me again, this time with her son in tow.

My sister blinks. "Wow, she tore out of here like a bat out of hell. What'd you do to piss her off?"

I scoff. "Nothing. She'll be back. We have plans to record for Red on Monday," I say, not wanting to reveal our weekend plans for a date.

"Don't tease her too much, okay? She did have a crush on you and it's not something she ever talked about," Gemma warns.

"You keep *saying* that, but what does it mean? She was like fourteen the last time I saw her," I insist, and Gemma stares at me.

"No, she wasn't. She was seventeen, and it was right after you and Maria broke up."

Now it's my turn to blink at Gemma. "Hell, that time in my life is like a haze. I don't remember anything from back then," I admit. "That makes a lot of sense."

Gemma shakes her head. "Yeah, you were a mess. So

don't tease her too much. I know you don't have time to get serious about anyone right now."

I nod slowly. "Yeah, of course not."

Getting serious about Zoe is *exactly* what I want to do, and I can't even deny it to myself anymore. She'd met me at a time when I was a complete shitshow, and I want to show her that I'm not that guy anymore. I don't care that she's Gemma's best friend, I'll take the ribbing from her just like I rib her and Locke about their relationship. She can't be a hypocrite, after all, since she's married to my best friend.

I think about telling her right now, but in the event that Zoe doesn't want me to, I keep my mouth shut. I'm going to wow Zoe on this date Friday night, and I can't wait.

I spill to the one person I know will keep my secret: Locke Kincaid. He won't tell Gemma no matter how much she tries to get him to, because his loyalty is to me at this point. After our fallout when he got Gemma pregnant, we've been thick as thieves, and Gemma is none the wiser.

"I need to talk to you," I tell Locke on the phone. "But I need Gemma out of the house."

"I've got Cain over at Axel and Harley's. Come over here and we can all jam."

I freeze. "Is Sam coming?" I ask coldly.

"No, he said he had something else planned already," Locke says.

"Good," I mumble, and when Locke asks what, I just brush it off.

I don't care if Axel and Harley find out, either. Axel's more loose-lipped and he's friends with Gemma, but I don't think he'll out me on something like this. The only person I would be a little concerned about is Samuel, and most of that is jealousy, to tell the truth. He's the one who's closest to Zoe, and I don't like that, that's all there is to it.

He's still my friend, of course, but for this matter I'm glad he won't be there.

I arrive at Axel and Harley's little duplex in about half an hour, and I'm met at the door by Cain in a bouncer, babbling incessantly.

"Yeah, buddy, seems like you had a hard day," I tease, and Cain babbles something back to me before focusing on bouncing and playing with his toys.

"He's a chatterbox like his mama," Locke groans.

Jasmine, on the other hand, is quieter, just rolling around in her crib and trying to grab for her toes, which I think is a milestone of some kind.

"Jazz is a quiet girl," I say, and Harley scoffs.

"Now she is. Once it's time to go to bed, she cries for Daddy and nothing else will do."

"She's a daddy's girl," Axel says, grinning, and Harley rolls her eyes.

"So, what's going on with you? You never ask to talk unless it's about a girl."

Axel sits up straighter. "Yes, spill, spill. Us, married men, have to live vicariously through your exploits." Harley hits him in the back of the head as she walks by and he flinches.

I clear my throat, suddenly regretting my decision to tell the friends that had been like my brothers all of these years.

I sit down on the couch next to Axel, sighing. "I'm sleeping with Gemma's best friend."

Locke's eyes bulge out of his head.

Axel stares at me. "The little stylist with the blue hair?"

"The very same," I say sagely, and Locke frowns at me, throwing a nearby object which happens to be a soft, squeaky baby toy,

"You cannot fuck Gemma's best friend!" he yells, and

Cain turns around to stare at him, not used to his father raising his voice. "What is this, some kind of weird payback?"

I flinch as he throws increasingly harder baby toys at me. "No! It's not revenge, it just... it happened while we were on tour, and I didn't recognize her, and now I *do* and it's just... it's a mess," I finish, and finally Locke stops throwing things at me.

"You *really* can't judge," Axel says to Locke, and I look at him, satisfied.

Locke groans. "Now I'll have to keep a secret from my wife. Do you know how hard that is?"

"I do," I say solemnly, "and I appreciate you. I owe you my life."

"Oh, shut up," Locke grumbles, but he's smiling.

"So, you're just sleeping with her or have you already fallen for her?" Axel asks.

I frown. "What's that supposed to mean?"

"You fall in love about as many times as I breathe in a month," Locke jokes, and Axel nods.

"Yeah, man, you and me, we're the same. Hopeless romantics," he says. "Locke was the true fuckboy, all this time."

"Not anymore. Now it's all on Samuel," Locke says.

"Stop talking about me like I'm not here," I complain. "And also, stop talking about me like I'm already married."

"Aren't you? Like in your head, have you already imagined your wedding?"

She'd wear blue, of course, and the flowers would be blue, and I'd call her baby blue in our wedding vows...

I shook my head. "No. Absolutely not," I lie.

"He *has*," Axel coos. "Tell me, what color suit are you going to wear?"

"Black, of course," I say instantly and then clap a hand over my mouth.

Locke bursts out laughing. "You're always like this, man, it's like once you meet a girl you like, it's game over."

"This is different. I *know* Zoe. I've known her for a long time. That's why I'm falling so fast."

Axel nods. "That might have something to do with it. Knowing Harley sure made me fall in love a lot quicker the second time."

"You never fell *out* of love with me, you big clown."

Axel grins goofily. "She's right. I didn't."

I smile at him, happy for him. I'm happy for both of them, I just... I want what they have. I want a wife and a family, and lately, I've been thinking maybe it should be Zoe. I did fall in love too quickly, fall too hard, but what's the problem with that? Zoe and I have known each other since we were kids, and maybe this time, falling in love is the right thing.

"So, what's the problem? Gemma will be pissed for only about five minutes, you know her," Locke offers.

I sigh. "It isn't just that. You know Zoe has a kid, and she's very protective of him. Plus, she's only committed to one date. She seems to think the thing with Gemma is a really big deal."

"It's gonna be fine," Axel waves it off. "Gemma gets mad quick, but she gets over it quick, too. She was only mad at Locke about five minutes the last fight they got into."

Locke stares at him. "She's different with me, man. She was mad three days; how do you not remember? I slept on *your* couch."

"Oh yeah," Axel chuckles. "But she won't be like that with Jackson."

"Nah, not with her big brother," Locke agrees.

I have to agree with them. Gemma feels like she owes me somehow for raising her, and even though I don't want that kind of payback, I do enjoy the things it lets me get away with. I think that this will be one of those things, where Gemma forgives me for sleeping with her best friend. At least, I hope so, because I have big plans.

"Where do I take her on our date?" I ask, and they both have plenty of ideas, talking over each other.

"A nice dinner," Locke says.

"Take her to a concert," Axel offers.

"Both of those are terrible ideas," Harley says, sitting down on Axel's lap.

His arms go around her easily and she leans back against him. That's what I want with Zoe, and I'm tired of being lonely. I'm tired of reaching out for someone each morning and no one being there. That's why I was so hurt when she left early the day after the concert.

"She likes music, right, she's an active girl," Harley says, "so take her to a roller rink."

I blink. "Oh my God. That might be the most perfect date idea ever. Axel, I'm going to kiss your wife."

"Only if you want to die," Axel says cheerfully, and I make do with just a hug.

"She used to love roller rinks when we were kids, always begging me to do the couples dance with her." I pause. "She really *did* have a crush on me, huh? I was just too stupid to know it."

"You're too stupid for a lot of things," Locke says dryly, and I throw some baby toys back at him.

We all end up in the garage, and we rehearse the melody to "Blue," the song I've written about Zoe.

"You really do have it bad," Axel says when we're done, and I have to admit he's right.

I want Zoe, and I plan on this date being the best one ever, so she'll want me back.

Chapter 10

Zoe

Picking you up at seven, baby blue.

I stare down at the text. It seems like the days leading up to us going out on a real date, something I'd actually agreed to, had gone by too fast. I don't even know what to *wear*, Elijah's being clingy because he's sick, and I'm of half a mind to call the whole thing off.

"You deserve a bit of fun, Suze," my mother says, refusing still to call me by my middle name. It doesn't bother me much.

"But Elijah's been sick," I hedge, and my mother glares at me.

"I took care of you enough times when you were sick that I think I know what I'm doing," she snaps, and she's right.

I do deserve a bit of fun, but I think if Mom knew it was with the father of my baby, she'd be less willing to watch Elijah.

Jackson had told me to dress casually, so I finally decided on a pair of boots with knee high socks and a black skirt with a red blouse. Red was my favorite color, after all, and I felt confident in the black skirt. I know Jackson loves my thighs and ass, and the skirt shows off both, after all.

Jackson picks me up at seven, just like he said he would, and he takes me to dinner at a nearby diner.

"This isn't all," he assures me. "We're going somewhere else you'll like a lot," he promises.

"I like this," I admit. It's one of those old-school fifties diners with the big jukebox playing big band music and swing, and I have to admit I love the rockstar themed menu.

I order a Billie Holliday shake and a Buddy Holly burger, and Jackson orders the same, smiling at me.

"How's the little guy?" he asks, and I sigh.

"He's still a little sickly. It's a stomach flu or something, it's been going around." I look up at him from under my eyelashes. "I almost didn't come."

Jackson frowns. "I would have understood, if he's still really sick."

I shake my head. "No, he's okay. I guess it was more mom guilt than anything else."

Jackson smiles. "You have a lot of that, don't you?"

"I do," I admit. "I guess it's because of not having his father around, like you said."

"I still say you deserve some fun," Jackson says firmly.

I realize how different this is from the first time we hooked up at his place when he was so drunk he could barely stand. He'd been a mess, his eyes bloodshot, and he's nothing like that, now. He doesn't even order a beer with dinner, and I have to admit that I'm proud of him.

"You still having fun?" I ask. "Even without the booze?"

Jackson snorts. "*Especially* without the booze. You know, when you didn't call me back when I got back in town, I went on a rager with Axel. I wanted to kill myself from the hangover alone, not to mention all the stupid shit we did. That was the last time I've drank, and I don't plan to again."

I smile. "That's a really smart decision, Jackson. It's not like you ever had a problem, exactly, but you definitely tended to overdo it sometimes."

"I do," he admits. "I got really into living the rockstar life, using it to numb certain shit in my personal life, but I don't want to do that anymore." He looks at me seriously. "I want to live my life. I want to feel everything, now."

"Even if it's bad?" I ask.

Jackson tilts his head. "Even if it's bad. Why do you ask? You gonna break my heart, baby blue?"

I flush, not used to that nickname in public. "I-I don't have plans to," I say. I think I would lose it if I ever really hurt Jackson. It's okay for him to hurt me, it always has been, but I definitely don't think I could do the same.

"Good." Jackson moves out of his side of the booth to sit in mine, squeezing me toward the window, and I look out of it, smiling.

This is dangerous, a voice in my head says. *You love him. You've always loved him, and this isn't helping matters.*

I shake my head to rid myself of those negative thoughts. I've been telling myself that I'm just going to enjoy this perfect moment, this moment that I've wanted ever since I was a kid.

What's the worst that can happen? It can be *too* perfect?

I guess that was the worry in the back of my head. What if it is too perfect and I can never say no to him again?

I finish eating my fries with Jackson's help, but I only manage half my burger. It's one of those big, half pound ones, and Jackson calls for a to-go box. He pays the bill just like a gentleman and holds my hand on the way back to the car.

It's pretty perfect, the voice warns. *And there's more?*

Surely, the more he's speaking about is just taking me back to his place where he'll make me a drink and he'll drink a soda, right? Surely, it'll just be sex, our second and final time since we decided.

"I need you to close your eyes," Jackson says softly, and I oblige, a little worried and biting at my cuticle. He takes my left hand so I won't bite it anymore, putting it on top of his on the gearshift.

My palms are sweating already. I could have never imagined a better scenario in my wildest dreams as a kid. Just holding his hand after he paid for a meal for me. The voice is right. This is bad.

We drive for a while and Jackson hums along with the radio and again, that voice in my head starts up.

Remember what happened last time? When everything was perfect?

Not now, I want to argue back. I don't want to remember that *now,* not when Jackson's trying so hard.

He sat up in bed after it was over, after he'd been snoring for the past two hours and I'd been staring at him, not believing that I'd just lost my virginity to the love of my life, Jackson Arden. I'd always thought he thought he was too good for me, hell, that's what I thought, after all. He was too old for me, my mother would have said, but I didn't care.

"Are you sick?" I asked him, rubbing his back, and he choked out a sob.

"Not the way you think," he'd said, and I sat up, frowning.

"What are you talking about, Jackson?" I asked, and then when he spoke, I wished I hadn't.

"She's gone," he sobbed. "Maria left me."

After every good thing that happened in his bed, after he held me and told me how beautiful I was, how sweet, he was crying over his ex-girlfriend while I was still naked, lying beside him.

I slowly move my hand away from Jackson's, the memory jolting me out of whatever reverie I had been in. The voice is right. I shouldn't be doing this. *But* I shouldn't be dating Jackson Arden for so many reasons. The biggest one because he broke my heart when I was seventeen years old.

I tell myself to calm down, to finish the date, and when Jackson tells me to open my eyes it's after he's walked me inside some kind of building. It's cool in the building and music travels to me faintly through speakers that must be embedded into the wall.

"Open," Jackson says, and we're standing in the middle of the roller rink, the same one that I'd begged him to hold my hand and do a couples dance with me. Once he'd done it, but he'd been so drunk he almost fell over.

I swallow hard, looking around. This is perfect. This is the re-do I want, but he doesn't know. He doesn't remember. He doesn't even know that we were together, back then. He'd been too fucked up to remember.

I can't do this.

I don't realize I've said it out loud until Jackson frowns, coming toward me.

"What do you mean? You don't like it, Zoe? We can go somewhere else—"

"No," I say, backing away. "I mean I can't do this. I can't go on this date with you. I'm sorry. I made the wrong decision."

I run out of the roller rink and around the corner,

breathing hard and waiting for him to come after me. When he does, I sneak around the other side of the building and schedule an Uber, hearing him curse.

I wince at the sound of it, but I can't help it. I've got to get home before I break down and tell him everything. If he figures out that we hooked up back then, it's only a matter of time before he figures out that Elijah's his, and I can't let that happen.

Jackson may have changed, but it's too little, too late.

Chapter 11

Jackson

Sure, I'd had my heart broken before. Pretty badly, in fact. But I don't think I've ever been completely and utterly rejected the way that Zoe Carmichael just did to me.

She left me right at the crux of the date, when I was trying to make up for all those years she crushed on me, and I didn't return her feelings. I really thought I was doing the right thing.

I just know this is a good idea. I know she'll love it, if I can just *find* her. She can't have gone far, after all. She isn't just going to run away, right? Where is she going to go?

When I make it around the back of the building, I see Zoe getting into an Uber and I call out her name, desperate.

She looks at me just once before averting her eyes, looking away from me like she can't bear the sight of me.

I stare after the car taking her away for the longest time, wondering what in the hell just happened. I've never been stood up before, never been ditched in the middle of a date like this. I know I'm a good-looking guy, so it definitely has to be my personality.

I don't remember ever being particularly mean to her when we were kids–am I forgetting something? I have the feeling I'm forgetting a lot of things, since during that time I was blacked out drunk every weekend. I managed to keep it together during the week, getting Gemma off to school, taking care of things, working two to three jobs to keep everything together, but every weekend, I felt like I needed a break.

The break consisted of me hanging out with Maria and us both drinking to excess, but at the time, I'd thought I was in love. I guess I had been, in the way that first loves were. She wasn't my first but I thought she'd be my last, and when she left me, I'd been devastated.

"It's too much, Jackson. We're always drunk or partying and I can't keep doing this. I can't keep living this rockstar lifestyle," she'd said.

"Maria, please," I begged. *"I'll be better. I'll change. I'll do anything."*

She paused. "It isn't just that, Jackson. You're always focused on Gemma, it's like she's your daughter instead of your little sister. I don't want a kid right now, we're kids ourselves. I just... I can't live your lifestyle and even if you do get it together, I can't be a stepmom."

I'd closed my mouth, despair washing over me in a wave, and I knew there was nothing I could do. I could change the drinking, the partying, but I could never change what Gemma meant to me, how I needed to protect her and take care of her, to raise her when my parents couldn't.

I'd been drunk for two months, nearly every day, after she left me, although I kept it to a few beers after work during the week.

I stand there, watching the empty spot on the road

where Zoe's Uber drove around the corner, and everything seems to wash over me in a wave.

Nothing lasts, something in my head tells me, some vile, mean voice that repeats the worst things over and over. *Nothing ever lasts, and you know that.*

Grief is a funny thing. It hits you when you're least expecting it. When you think you've moved on, when it's been years and years, suddenly it hits you and it's all you can think about. *Nothing lasts forever.*

Nothing lasts at all, I think, going back into the roller rink to cancel the spot I'd reserved. I look longingly over at the concession table, the cold beer they're advertising, but I don't want to go backward. I just want to go forward, and I want to go forward with Zoe.

Nonetheless, though, I want a drink. I want something to blur out all the edges of what I'm feeling, of how this makes me feel like Maria breaking up with me all over again. I call the closest thing I have to a sponsor: my sister.

"Jack? What's wrong?" she answers.

"I need to come over," I say hoarsely, and she hums in the back of her throat.

"I just put Cain to bed. Are you okay?"

"No," I manage.

"Hurry," she says. "He won't sleep forever."

"I'll be there in fifteen."

I show up to Gemma's house wearing my silk shirt, looking like I'm going somewhere fancy, but I've unbuttoned a few buttons of the top, feeling like the collar is choking me. I feel *awful,* maybe more awful than I've felt in years, and I don't even know what I'm going to tell Gemma about it.

"Have you been drinking?" she asks me, first thing, and

I want to be irritated but I know that it's coming from a place of love and concern.

I shake my head. "No, but I damn sure want to," I mumble, plopping down on the couch.

Gemma sits across from me in the chair. "What happened? Why are you all dressed up?"

"I was on a date."

Gemma's eyes widen. "A *date*? You haven't been on a real date since... Laura or whatever her name was."

"Lena," I correct her. "And this is different."

Gemma rolls her eyes. "You always say that."

I wince. I can always count on Gemma to tell me the truth, even if it's something I don't want to hear.

"I'm serious this time, Gem. This girl means a lot to me, and I don't know why it went so wrong."

"Where did you take her? What happened? You're not giving me enough information, Jackson."

"Stop with the third degree! Calm down, I'll get to it," I said irritably, trying to think of how I can skirt around who it is while giving her all the information.

I sigh. "I met her on tour."

Gemma narrows her eyes. "I *knew* you were sneaking around with somebody."

"Just a little," I say with a grin. "But it wasn't serious, at least not at first. Once I got to know her, I wanted to know more about her, and I asked her out for real. She said no about a million times, but eventually, I wore her down."

"As you do," Gemma says, laughing a little.

"I know she likes me," I say firmly, "I know she does because she's *told* me."

"Then what *happened*?" Gemma asks, exasperated.

"We had a great dinner, and then I took her to a roller

rink and she just... ghosted me. She said she couldn't do this and sprinted outside, took an Uber home."

Gemma stares at me for a moment. "What did you do?"

"What do you *mean* what did I do? I didn't do anything!"

"You must have done *something*," she insists. "If not, there was no reason for her to leave."

I took in a deep breath through my nostrils and rubbed a hand across my face.

"I can't tell you."

"What do you mean you can't tell me?" Gemma hits my shoulder with the heel of her hand. "I'm your *sister*, you tell me everything!"

"You don't tell *me* everything, since you fucked my best friend without telling me," I shoot back, and Gemma groans.

"Are you really still not over that?"

I pout. "No. We're supposed to be best friends."

"We *are* best friends, Jack, but I knew you'd be weird about it and plus, I didn't even know how I felt about him at the time," Gemma explains.

I'm not really still upset about it, but it's fun to tease her. Especially since now, I'm in a similar situation, sleeping with her best friend and lying about it. I can finally see her point of view now, and I feel sort of bad about keeping it from her.

"It's not just about a girl," I tell her. "It's just that plus the tour, the album–I've been under a lot of stress," I hedge, and Gemma glares at me but she seems to buy it.

"Maybe you should let go of this girl, then, Jackson," Gemma says gently. "You know how you get wrapped up in relationships, and I need you sharp for the tour."

"I'm sharp," I insist. "Sharp as a tack. I just had a bad

night, that's all. I assume she never wants to talk to me again, anyway."

"Again, I can't help you unless you tell me what you did wrong."

"I don't even know what I did wrong," I say honestly. "I thought she'd really like going to the roller rink, she always did when...." I pause, noticing my mistake. "When we first started."

"You took her roller skating on tour?"

I shrug. "Ice skating," I lie, and Gemma seems to take it at face value.

It's hard to lie to my sister, and I wonder how she did it all those weeks on tour when she was seeing Locke. Maybe Gemma is sneakier than I am.

"If she ditched you during a date, she seems like kind of a bitch," Gemma says, never one to mince words. "Maybe you should just let it go."

"Maybe," I mumble, but the very idea of letting it go makes me feel terrible. Especially since Zoe will be accompanying us on tour, at least flying out for each concert to style us.

"All you can do is do what you always do, Jack—focus on your music."

That's easy enough for Gemma to say. Zoe is an integral part of all of my music, especially since I'd written a song for her, and she'll be there every step of the tour.

Chapter 12

Zoe

Going back into Jackson's studio for the final recording of "Red" is about the last thing I want to do, especially given that it's a song about Maria, his ex from back when I had a crush on him.

I guess I must have blocked that part out in my head, because the other day, on our date, was the first time I'd thought about it in years.

That's when I first realized how stupid I am and always have been about Jackson Arden, because even after that, I wanted him. He's the only man I've ever wanted, and the only man I've ever been with, so I guess it's no wonder.

Maybe I should get back out there. Maybe I should stop seeing Jackson, wait until after the tour, and start dating again. Surely the best way to get over someone was to get with someone else, right? I can't even imagine dating anyone else, but I guess maybe it's time.

First, though, I have to get through this final recording with Jackson, and this tour. So, I put on my big girl panties and take Elijah to my mother's, since he's still feeling a little off. Bless my mother for not asking why my eyes are so puffy when I drop him off. Maybe she thinks it's from lack of sleep from being up with Elijah all night.

When I knock on the studio door, it takes a long moment for Jackson to come to the door. When he does, he looks away from me almost immediately, something flashing across his face.

"Jackson," I start, but he ignores me, going into the soundproof booth and putting his headphones on.

I follow and he nods for me to sit next to him. He plays what he's recorded of "Red" and it's soulful, emotional, just how I knew it would be, and the rawness in his voice almost brings tears to my eyes.

He cared about her. For all I know, he still does. The way it sounds certainly makes me feel like it, and I think I made the right decision leaving in the middle of our date, even though I still feel some amount of guilt about it.

He had looked so sad, shoulders slumped, head tilted in confusion, when I'd ridden away, but I just couldn't go through with it. It brought back too many bad memories. Too many memories of me wanting him, loving him, and him barely noticing me. And even when he did... well, that didn't go well, either, not in the end.

I hadn't just made the decision not to tell him because I thought he was too much of a mess to be a dad, even though that was part of it. I made the decision not to tell him about Elijah because I knew he didn't love me. Not like he loved Maria. I don't ever want to be anyone's second choice.

I close my eyes and focus on singing the backup vocals, and it comes out good, all the raw emotion I feel from how Jackson had treated me that first day after, and when I open my eyes, tears are streaming down my face.

Jackson looks at me and there's something in his green eyes that I can't name, that I can't put my finger on.

He gets up, taking off his headphones and marching into the other room, beckoning me to follow.

"What's up?" I ask, wiping at my face. "It wasn't good?"

"It was amazing," he snaps. "It's always amazing but I can't do this right now. I need you to go."

"Wh-what do you mean you need me to go? Are we finished?"

"We're finished," he says stonily. "We're finished for good."

"What is that supposed to mean?" I ask, panic rising in my throat.

"You *left* me," he says in a low, hoarse voice. "I set up this big date for us and you just left me standing like a jerk in the parking lot. You know that's the first time I've ever been stood up?"

"I'm sorry, Jackson, look, you don't understand." I fumble for an excuse, not wanting this to be over even if I know it should be. "Elijah's been sick and the sitter–"

"Don't lie to me," Jackson warns, taking a few steps toward me. "I hate it when you lie to me. Elijah's a great kid, if he wasn't feeling well you know that I would have understood. Hell, I would have come over and brought him chicken soup and watched cartoons with him, Zoe."

I scoff, more tears welling in my eyes. "We don't have that kind of relationship."

"What kind of relationship do we have, then? One where I fuck you in club bathrooms and in my studio? Is that the kind of relationship you want?" He nearly yells and I back up again, hitting the corner of the couch.

"Isn't that the kind of relationship *you* want? That's how we met, hooking up, you sneaking me around because you were *ashamed* of me."

"I was never ashamed of you. Don't put fucking words into my mouth, Zoe."

"You don't understand how it made me feel. You don't understand how you always make me feel," I say, my voice liquid.

"Tell me, then," he says softly, getting closer, putting his hand on my cheek and caressing my jaw. "Tell me how I make you feel."

"Crazy," I whisper. "Like I'm sixteen again looking up to my best friend's older brother and wanting him. Never being able to have him."

"You have me now, Zoe. You've got me, if you just wanted me. Tell me you don't want me if you don't, Zoe, because I feel just as crazy as you do," Jackson pleads, searching my face with those gorgeous green eyes of his.

"I do want you," I say, unable to lie even as tears stream down my face. "I want you so bad, and I always have."

"I want you too," Jackson says hoarsely. "So bad, Zoe. I want you so bad."

My lip is trembling but I press my mouth to his anyway, kiss him hard and hungry,

Jackson takes hold of my hips in his hands, turns me around so that I'm bent over the couch arm.

"Is this how you want me?" he asks. "You just want me inside you and nowhere else? Don't want to be seen with me, don't want me to take you on dates, just want me to fuck you in my studio like I'm your dirty little secret?"

"No," I gasp, but I'm not sure if he hears me because his hands are already sliding down my pants. "I want you any way I can get you," I finish, and he hears that because he lets out a long moan.

"If this is all I can get, I'll take it, because I can't stop thinking about you, Zoe," he murmurs. "I think about your lips and your eyes and this pussy..." He slides his fingers into me, slowly at first and then pumping faster, angling his fingers up, scissoring his fingers to stretch me.

"Oh, God, Jackson," I breathe, and he takes that as encouragement, and that's good, because it is, I'm already spreading my legs.

One more time, I tell myself. *A goodbye of sorts.* I tell myself that I want it differently than this, that I wish that it was soft and sweet instead of rough, but part of me craves this, part of me wants it just like this, just like the first time when we hooked up in a club.

I love the way he touches me, the way he hisses when he pushes into me, how hard he fucks me, making me hold on to the leather couch cushions so hard my knuckles turn white as he propels me forward.

He grabs two handfuls of my ass, spreading me apart to get deeper, and when I look behind me he's looking at where he's entering me and nearly pulling out, ramming back into me.

"You like it like this, don't you, baby blue? You like it hard and rough, like to be fucked so hard you can't think?"

"Yes," I moan, and it's true, I love the way I can't think of anything but him, how I'm surrounded by his scent and his touch and everything about him. It's what I've wanted my whole life, but I just want more than he can give me.

I reach my orgasm quickly, but Jackson doesn't stop, keeps fucking me hard and fast and I make a guttural sound from the back of my throat when I come again.

"You'll leave me when this is over," he says softly, and I go silent, only the sounds of my heavy breathing in the room and the lewd squelching of our lovemaking.

"No," I whisper, but I don't think he hears me. He pulls me up by my waist, forcing me to go onto my tiptoes while he thrusts up beneath me, and it's like the whole world is made of Jackson, just him and me in this bubble and nothing else matters.

I don't want it to be over. I don't want it ever to be over, but I know it has to be, I know that eventually, he'll spill inside me and then I'll have to go, have to try and forget about him, at least until we go on tour and I have to fly out for the important shows.

Dallas. Montgomery. Atlanta. Those are the three big ones that Gemma wants me to fly out for, and they span over six weeks. Two shows each and then it'll be over and I won't ever have to see Jackson Arden again.

My heart feels broken even as I try to focus on how good my body feels, how his hands go up to my breasts, his palms skidding over my nipples which are hard beneath the fabric of my tank top.

"I want more than this," he tells me. "I want all of you, Zoe Carmichael."

It's what I've wanted to hear from him my entire life. It was my life's goal before I even got into fashion, into styling. I want a family with Jackson Arden, and the universe had given me one, but in the cruelest way. I can never tell him. He'll hate me forever, and he might hate Elijah by extension, resent him because he resents me.

I love you, I think, when he finally grunts out my name and comes inside me. *I'll always love you, Jackson.*

He pulls out of me too abruptly and I whine at how empty I feel but he doesn't seem to notice, pulling my pants back up harshly and stepping away, adjusting himself back into his sweats.

"Now, you can go," he says harshly, and I stare at him for a long moment.

"Is that what you want?" I ask softly.

He won't look at me. "That's what you want. I'm giving you what you want, Zoe. One last time, right? That was our second. You can be done now."

Tears well in my eyes and I try to keep them from streaming down my cheeks.

"We're not good for each other, Jackson. This is the only way."

"Get out, then," he says firmly, and goes into the sound-proof booth, not even looking at me as I walk outside and burst into tears.

Chapter 13

Jackson

I can't bear to be in the studio anymore, not when it smells like her everywhere, so I go home instead of going to the bar like I want to. I'm keeping it together by the skin of my teeth, but at least she's never been to my place, so maybe I won't think of her as much.

It doesn't work. I fall asleep too early, around nine, and all I can do is dream of her.

"You're so beautiful," I told her, and my words come too slow. I felt like I was stuck in glue, my hands fumbling with the buttons of her blouse.

"You are," she said, and there were stars in her blue eyes. Her hair was long and dark, not the short blue bob it was later.

I chuckled. "I don't know about that."

My hands ran down her sides, her hips.

She swallowed hard, looking up at me with those piercing blue eyes of hers.

"What are you doing, Jackson?" I asked, and I tried to focus on her face although it was hard for some reason.

"Do you want me, Susie Q?" I asked her, and she gasped,

her lower body leaning toward mine, her hands going up to my chest.

"Do you want me?" she asked in the smallest voice.

"Of course I do," I mumbled, "look at you. All hips and thighs in this little dress of yours. I want you so bad."

"Don't say that, Jack. Not if you don't mean it," she whispered, and I took her hand and pressed it against my crotch, thrusting into her palm.

Her blue eyes opened wide. "You do want me," she said throatily, and that was all I needed.

I leaned down and kissed her, hard, my head spinning, my teeth gnashing against hers. It was sloppy and I felt light-headed, although I didn't know if it was from the booze or the way her skin felt smooth beneath my palms.

Her breasts were just bigger than a handful, my fingers twisting at her nipples as soon as I got that dress off her, and then she was lying on my bed, just in her panties, knees up and legs spread open. She was wearing this little pair of cotton panties that were soaked at the crotch.

"Susie," I whispered. "Let me taste you."

I woke up before I pressed my face against her sex, again panting and hard in my sweats. *What the fuck is this dream I keep having?* I thought, but then it slowly began to dawn on me. That wasn't a dream. It wasn't a dream at all, it was *real*.

I'd hooked up with Zoe, then known as Susie, back when she was seventeen. Jesus Christ, she had been jailbait, or at least I'd viewed her as that, but the last time we saw each other she was just a couple months away from her eighteenth birthday in October. No wonder Zoe is mad. Not only had I not recognized her from when we were younger, I forgot that we hooked up.

How long had that been, four, five years ago? God, I'm

an idiot. I sit straight up in bed and rub my hands across my face. I had to get in the shower and find Zoe, apologize for everything. I take the most half-assed shower of my life and towel myself off.

I throw on a pair of fresh jeans and a T-shirt that smells like it's been washed at least a few days ago and jump in my beat-up car to head to Zoe's apartment. The only reason I even know where to go is because I'd picked her up from here on our date. I knock on the door once, and when no one answers, I knock again, and a man answers the door.

He's a smaller guy, looks a little older than me with silver around his temples, but he's not quite old enough to be her father.

I narrow my eyes at him. "Who are you?"

"Who the hell are *you?*" he snaps back.

"I'm Zoe's... friend," I say, biting back the word *boyfriend.*

"She's not here; she's at the store," he says, and I want to push past him inside, see if she's hiding in there, but why would she be? I have no claim on her, as much as I want to, but *who the hell is this guy?*

It's already driving me crazy. I can't believe I'm standing here, staring down some guy in Zoe's apartment, but what else am I supposed to do?

"I'll wait," I say in a clipped voice, and he shrugs.

"You can wait in the car," he says, and slams the door in my face.

I stalk back to the car and immediately pull my phone out to call Zoe. She doesn't answer, which I'm not surprised by given how we ended things the last time we'd seen each other. I'd been too rough and cold with her, even though all I'd been trying to do was tell her how hurt I was that she'd stood me up.

I scroll up to Locke's contact, knowing that Gemma will be out and about getting things ready for us to leave on Friday. She'll be renting the van and booking tickets and even if she's at home, she'll be busy in their little home office.

"The baby just went to sleep so if your call woke him up I'm going to kill you," Locke answers dryly.

"Has he been having sleeping issues lately? Gemma said basically the same thing to me," I ask, and then pause, shaking my head. "Never mind. More importantly, tell me not to dropkick this asshole in Zoe's apartment."

"Wait, what? You're at Zoe's apartment and she's not there? What are you, stalking her?"

"No," I say through gritted teeth. "I just came over because I realize I'm a moron and I wanted to apologize."

"Apologize about what? Didn't she stand you up?"

"Yes, but—" I sigh. "I think I hooked up with her when she was a kid and forgot about it."

"Ah, Jesus, Jackson, she's so much younger than you!"

"You are literally the least qualified person to judge me," I warn, and Locke groans.

"Okay, okay, you're right. So what, when she was seventeen, eighteen, you guys hooked up? And you *forgot*? How do you forget a whole hookup, Jackson?"

"It was after me and Maria broke up!" I say defensively. "I was drunk like ninety percent of the time for a month, and I think that was just a couple days after."

"But still, a whole hookup? What happened?"

I think about it for a long moment and vaguely remember Zoe rubbing my back, telling me everything was going to be okay. I feel all the blood drain from my face.

"I think I cried about Maria when we were in bed together," I wince, and Locke chokes on air.

"Oh my *God,* that's the worst thing I've ever heard," Locke says, snorting out a laugh. "Maybe you didn't even close the deal, if you were that drunk—"

"God, that's even worse," I groan. "This is terrible, and now some fucking *guy* is at her apartment, and I don't know what to do."

"What *are* you doing?"

I look at the apartment. "Uh, kind of staking the place out to see when she gets back," I admit.

"Jackson, you *are* an idiot. Get out of there, and *don't* ask her about the guy."

"What do you *mean* don't ask her about the guy? If she's living with some asshole—"

"Jackson, trust me. Jealousy will get you nowhere. Gemma likes it when I'm possessive but when I get jealous I'm an asshole, and I know you are too."

I huff out a breath. "Maybe," I mumble.

"Definitely," Locke says. "Please, for once in your life, take my advice."

"I'll try," I say, but I keep staring at the window, wondering what's going on in there. Is she inside and just avoiding me? Has she had a boyfriend this whole time? I'm quiet for a long time on the line.

"Jackson?" Locke calls.

"Yeah?"

"Stop spiraling. I can basically hear you freaking out."

"I'm not freaking out," I complain. I definitely *am* freaking out. I am *most definitely* freaking out. I hooked up with Zoe when she was a teenager, back when she'd been Susie, and I'd forgotten all about it even though I'd cried about my ex *in bed with her.*

How much worse could things get?

"Before you freak out, come over. We'll go out to The Dirty Dozen and–shit, you can't drink," Locke says.

"And you've got the baby," I remind him.

"I'll take him over to the sitter," Locke says. "Gemma's out all day getting things together, anyway. We'll go to the Dirty Dozen and listen to music and *not drink*. Just get our mind off things."

I nod, feeling slightly better. There is a reason that Locke Kincaid is my best friend, after all. "Okay. Meet you there in an hour."

"Don't spend that hour staking out her apartment, you psycho."

"Absolutely not," I say, but after hanging up, that's exactly what I do.

Zoe doesn't come home and the guy doesn't leave, so I head over to The Dirty Dozen.

Chapter 14

Zoe

My mother and my sister have gotten into some big fight, and since Georgia is a couple years older than me but nowhere near as mature, I'd offered her a place to stay for a few days. I keep taking Elijah to daycare, though, because Georgia is *hopeless* with kids, plus I assume her jerk of a boyfriend will be coming over. He's twice her age and somehow less mature than she is.

I assume that's what she and mom fought about, but the problem is that I'm supposed to meet Gemma and Elijah's still sick. I'm at my mom's place begging him to climb off my hip when Gemma calls. I'm half an hour late and already freaking out.

"Hey, Zo. I was getting worried, where are you?" she asks.

"Elijah's sick and clingy and I'm trying to get him to stay at my mom's," I say quickly. "Don't worry, I'll be able to peel him off me soon. My car's acting up, too, so I'll need to take an Uber."

"Don't do that," Gemma says easily. "I'll come pick you

up in the tour van. I wanted to show it to you anyway, I just rented it. Your mom still live in the same place?"

"Y-yeah," I stumble over my words, worried about her seeing Elijah. Surely, by the time she gets here, I can get him playing with my mom or something.

My mom does her level best, but Elijah is still crying when Gemma arrives. I make it almost to the door, Gemma smiling at me on the front door step with the screen door closed and the front door open, when Elijah comes running up behind me, grabbing me around the legs and wailing.

"Mama, I don't want you to go to work," he whines. "I want you to stay here. M'sick. You gotta take care of me."

"Grandma is gonna take care of you, honey," I tell him, trying to turn him around so Gemma can't see him.

"Oh, look at him! Is this the little guy?" Gemma asks, and finally I sigh, picking Elijah up and kissing him on the cheek. The jig is up. Either she'll figure it out, or she won't. Elijah looks right at her, sniffling.

Gemma smiles, taking him in, and I slowly see recognition pass across her face.

"Oh my God, Zoe," she says in a low tone, and my mother comes to rescue me, taking Elijah and distracting him with his favorite movie, Big Hero 6.

"He's cute, right?" I say wanly, hoping that she hasn't noticed as much as I think she's noticed.

Gemma is uncharacteristically quiet as we get into the tour bus, and I chatter on and on about how great the bus is.

"It's so big! Do you guys sleep in here?"

"The guys do, sometimes," Gemma says, sounding far away.

I pause, waiting for her to say something else, but she doesn't.

"Gemma?"

She abruptly pulls over onto the side of the road, flipping on the flashers and turning to me.

"Zoe, why does your son have my eyes?" she demands.

"I-I don't know. You know, genetics are weird..." I trail off, knowing that she knows.

"This has nothing to do with how you were obsessed with my brother for most of our teen years and how you suddenly left town one night? Zoe, I'm not an idiot. He's what, four? That means that you hooked up when you were about to turn eighteen...oh my God, I'm an aunt," Gemma says all in a rush, talking fast.

"Gemma, please," I plead. "Don't jump to conclusions. The guy I was with just happened to have green eyes."

Gemma narrows her eyes at me. "You're wearing your lying face, Zoe."

"I don't have a lying face!" I protest.

"Yes, you do. Your nose gets all wrinkly and your eyes go all wide and innocent," Gemma almost yells. "I've known you all of our lives, Susanne Zoe Carmichael, and I know when you're lying!"

"Okay, okay," I say finally, defeated and looking away. "Elijah is Jackson's. Are you happy?"

"*No*, I'm not happy! How could you have hidden this from him? How could you have hidden this from *me*?" Gemma sounds betrayed, and I feel guilty.

I cover my face with my hands, trying not to cry. "I know, Gemma, I *know*. It's just that it was just one time, and I knew Jackson was still hung up on that Maria chick, and you know how he was then. He was a mess, and I didn't think he was ready to be a dad."

Gemma pauses before taking my hands from my face, turning my chin so I have to look at her.

"You're right. You're right, Zo, he was a mess. He wasn't

ready to be a father, not then. But he's changed. Can't you see how much he's changed? I know that you don't have a thing for him anymore, maybe you've got someone else—"

I don't correct her, just listen.

"But Jackson would love to know Elijah. He'd love to be a father. He's so good with Cain..." she trails off, smiling. "And I'd love to be an aunt."

"I don't know," I say shakily. "I've kept it a secret for so long, and I don't know how to tell him. He'll hate me for keeping it a secret."

"He won't hate you, Zoe. Jackson doesn't have it in him to hate anyone, you know that. He has the biggest heart," she insists. "I'm kind of mad at you, but that doesn't mean that I hate you."

I sniffle, smiling at her. "Thanks for not hating me, Gem."

She huffs. "I would have if you'd never told me. At least you came clean before the kid was eighteen. Now he can get to know his Aunt Gemma and cousin Cain, at least."

"Slow down," I tell her. "I don't know if I'm ready for all that. He doesn't think he has a father."

Gemma frowns. "Are you trying to tell me that you were *never* going to tell Jackson? Even knowing that he's a different person now? A better person?"

I shake my head. "I don't know, Gemma. I thought maybe it was best not to complicate things."

Gemma sighs and bangs her head on the steering wheel. "One thing I learned losing my parents so young is this, Zoe. Complicate things. Mess things up. Take risks. Because you never know when your time is up."

I think about it for a long moment, looking at her. "So you think I should tell him?"

Gemma rolls her eyes. "Of *course* I think you should tell him. You have to tell him."

"And if I don't?" I ask, willing her to say she'll keep my secret."

Gemma looks at me stonily. "I will. I'll tell him and he'll be even more hurt that he had to learn it from someone else."

I take in a deep breath. "Can you give me some time?"

Gemma nods after a long pause. "Until the tour is over. It'll really mess with his head, that's for sure, and I don't want to spend all this money just for this to be a bust. So you have six more weeks. Twelve more shows, and only four of those you'll be working with Jackson. You're done with all the album stuff, yeah?"

I nod slowly. "Yeah, I think so."

We had only done a little recording the last time I'd been there, but I think we finished up, at least. It isn't like I can tell Gemma that we'd been fucking instead of going over our recordings.

She nods. "Okay. Well then, you tell him after the last show, it'll be in Albuquerque so it's near to home."

I should be panicking, but instead, I feel almost like I've got a weight lifted off my shoulders. I'd spent four years keeping this secret, four years telling lies to everyone I know, and now at least one person knows. Telling Jackson might be the hardest thing I ever have to do, but at least I have some time to think about how to do it.

"Now," Gemma says, as if I haven't dropped the biggest bomb ever on her shoulders. "Let's get to work."

Chapter 15

Jackson

The Dirty Dozen is packed with people, and both Locke and Axel show up. We order wings and sodas, all of us not used to drinking anymore.

"This feels kind of lame," Axel says, and I snort.

"Why, because we're usually three sheets to the wind by the time the wings come?"

Axel shrugs. "Yeah. I guess we're like, old married guys now."

"Speak for yourself," I mumble.

"So, are you gonna tell Axel why you're an idiot?" Locke asks, and I groan.

"Can Axel keep his big fat mouth shut?" I ask.

"I kept my mouth shut about your sister getting knocked up by Locke," he retorts, and I think about pushing him out of his chair but I restrain myself.

"Fine. So, it turns out I hooked up with Zoe when we were younger, and I forgot about it."

Axel stares at me. "You what?"

"I hooked up with—"

He cuts me off. "No, I mean you *forgot* about it? How?"

"I was drunk," I say glumly.

"Maria drunk," Locke tells Axel.

Axel's eyes widen. "*Ohhh*, so you were like me right after Harley left me drunk. That makes sense. I don't know what I did the whole first month."

"You get it," I say, pointing at him, and Locke shakes his head. He's always been a bit of a teetotaler, except for on rare occasions on tour when he had a bit too much to drink.

"So, she's mad that you didn't remember," Axel says. "That makes sense."

He tears into the wings, dipping one into blue cheese. I wrinkle my nose. I'm more of a ranch kind of guy, but to each his own.

"I guess," I say. "She hasn't explicitly said it."

Locke scoffs. "Of course she didn't. She wants you to remember on your own."

"How was I supposed to remember on my own? It's been nearly five years ago, and I was in a really bad place. Surely she knows that. Besides, she hooked up with me anyway, so what does that say?"

"That she likes you," Axel says, sucking the wing sauce off his fingers. "That maybe she's forgiven you, but she still wants you to remember."

"I *do* remember, kind of," I mumble, and Locke raises an eyebrow.

"Why does that sound like you remember more than you told me?"

I groan. "I think that I might have been upset about Maria after we finished," I explain.

"What do you mean by upset?" Axel asks, staring at me.

"Like... I think maybe she comforted me about Maria," I say in a low voice, and they both groan loudly.

"You *ass*," Locke says.

"You *idiot,*" Axel says at the same time.

"I know! I know, you're both right, but now I don't know what to say to her."

"You say you're sorry for being a giant asshole when she was a kid. You explain that you were a mess but that you're in a better place now," Axel advises, and I give him a look.

"That's... shockingly good advice, coming from you."

He shrugs. "I basically had to tell Harley that same thing. I had to apologize for the guy I was and convince her that I was gonna be a different guy in the future."

I frown. "That sounds too easy."

"It's not easy, believe me," Axel says. "I had to work really hard to convince her."

"I don't know if she'll buy it," I mutter. "She stood me up the other night, left me right in the middle of a date, and I still don't know what all that was about."

"She's probably just worried that you're still that same guy," Locke suggests.

"You think so?"

Axel nods, too. "Yeah, I mean that was the deal with Harley. She thought I was still some rock star flirting with girls, when in reality, I just wanted her."

"We *are* rock stars flirting with girls," I tell Axel, and he grins.

"Yeah, but it's just flirting. It's not like we're hooking up with them."

"I was," Locke says, smiling slyly, and I give him a look.

"Not anymore. You're a kept man and you know it."

Locke tilts his head. "I know it better than you."

"So you like Zoe? Like wanna marry her like her?" Axel asks, and my throat gets tight.

I swallow hard. "I don't know. Marriage is a strong word."

I can picture her in a white dress with a blue ribbon around her waist to match her eyes, but I'm not about to say that to the guys. They'll give me attitude forever about falling too fast.

"But you want to date her, right? Not just hook up?"

"Yes, of course. I want us to be together," I said firmly.

"What about that guy you saw at her house? Is she seeing someone else?" Axel asks.

Locke nudges him, but it's too late, a dark cloud has already washed over me.

"I dunno," I mumble.

"What if he's the father of the kid?" Axel continues, oblivious. "Like, just coming to visit or whatever."

I grit my teeth. "I guess it could be, but she said he wasn't in the picture."

"I always thought about that with Harley, you know, before she told me that Jazz was mine. I thought about what I'd do when the dad wanted back in the baby's life," Axel says, munching on fries.

"What would you have done?" Locke asks.

"I would have lost my fucking mind," Axel says cheerfully. "I have no idea what I would have done but I assume it would have ended with me in jail, like that time with her friend."

"Great, Ax, that's super helpful," I say dryly.

"Listen," Locke says, leaning forward. "You know she has a kid. You know that kid has a dad, so at some point, you've got to be okay with him being around at least the kid. She's not sleeping with the guy, right?"

"I don't know," I admit. "I hope not."

"What happens if she is?" Axel looks at me curiously.

"I'll lose my fucking mind," I echo him, and he starts to laugh, nearly spitting wings everywhere.

"I guess we're all possessive fucks," Locke laughs and I nod, smiling a little.

"I want her and everything that comes along with her, so if that includes an asshole baby daddy, so be it," I finally say, determined. "I want to make her happy, so I won't put more stress on her by being awful about it."

"That's a good way to look at it." Locke claps me on the back. "I couldn't take it if any of Gemma's exes were around."

"Gemma doesn't really have any exes," I say, musing. "Except for that one Jason guy she used to make out with every summer."

Locke's eyes shoot to mine. "Jason who?"

I bark out a laugh. "Shut up, I'm not telling you."

Locke grumbles but takes it in stride and we order nachos since Axel has decimated most of the wings.

I look at the beer menu, but ultimately decide that I'm not in the right space to even have one, and so I order another coke with grenadine.

"So ultimately, you just have to talk to her," Locke finishes, and I nod.

"Until then, can we just eat and watch the game?" I ask. And they both grin and nod.

"We're dads, we welcome any excuse to get out of the house," Axel says, and Locke agrees.

We end up staying out late and taking tons of pictures for social media, one or two with a few female fans.

Harley calls Axel, asking him about the girls in the pictures, but he can't stop grinning while he teases her about it.

Gemma, apparently, doesn't even bat an eye, because Locke doesn't get a single text.

"She trusts you," I say when he pouts. "That's a good thing."

"Yeah, I guess. She flirts a lot more than I do. I hate it when she goes out without me," he admits.

"She just thinks it's fun to rile you up, dude." That's one of Gemma's secrets, but surely he knows.

Locke blinks at me. "Really? I'm going to get her back."

"Oh? We need to find some groupies?" Axel asks slyly. "I'm good at that."

Axel brings a group of blondes over and a couple of them agree to sit on Locke's lap to take pictures, but Gemma *still* doesn't call him.

I laugh, shaking my head, and head over to the bar to get another coke with grenadine, but someone dancing spills a beer on my shirt and I curse.

"I'm so sorry, man," the guy mourns, but I just wave my hands dismissively. It's just a T-shirt, after all.

"What the hell do you think you're doing?" I hear my sister screech from a few yards away, and I turn around, grinning, to see her standing there with Zoe, who's looking at me with a frown, her nose wrinkled in disgust.

"Zoe," I say, taking a few steps toward me, and she takes a few steps back.

"You smell like a brewery," she snaps, and storms outside.

I sigh heavily.

Goddamnit.

Chapter 16

Zoe

"**W**hat the hell does Locke Michael Kincaid think he's doing?" Gemma screeches, and I jolt, nearly spilling my glass of wine.

It's late, nearing midnight, but my mother said that Elijah fell asleep hours ago and Gemma and I have been talking after shopping, so I figured a couple of glasses and some time with my best friend wouldn't hurt.

"We aren't picking up Cain until tomorrow morning," Gemma tells me. "Locke wanted a boys night out, but look at this picture!"

The picture *is* suggestive, but I can see that Locke isn't actually touching any of them, he's just got a hand steadying one of the girls perched on her knee and grinning.

I laugh. "He's just trying to piss you off."

"It's working," she fumes. She slams her glass of wine down. She's only had one, so she grabs the keys to the tour bus and jerks her head toward the door.

"Come on, Gemma. Locke would never cheat on you," I tell her, and she chuckles darkly.

"He knows I'd kill him if he did," she says seriously, and I blink at her.

"Gem, you're scaring me a little," I say with a nervous laugh.

She grins at me. "Let's go, I'm about to go tear my husband a new one," she says, and I giggle, just a little tipsy, and follow her.

When we arrive, I'm surprised to see Jackson's car there, but I figure he goes out with the guys a lot. I'm not sure that I want to see him, but Gemma drags me inside, nonetheless.

Jackson's standing there and instantly I see that he's disheveled, his shirt wet, and he smells like beer.

I snap at him and storm out, and he follows me outside.

I whirl around. "What do you want, Jackson? Last time we saw each other you told me to get out!"

Jackson huffs out a breath. "You told me we could only be together one last time, what was I supposed to do?"

"You were supposed to ask me to stay," I say quietly, so quietly I'm not sure he heard me.

Jackson takes a step toward me. "I wanted to, Zoe, but I was just... I was upset. You stood me up, for God's sake."

"I had my reasons," I snap back, and he heaves a sigh.

"I know that you did, baby blue. I remember."

"Wh-what?" He remembers? What does he remember?

"I remember our first time," he says softly, getting closer to me. "I remember maybe I was a jerk afterward."

I take a step back, my back resting against the tour bus.

"What do you mean *maybe*? You were totally a jerk. You cried about her right after you *fucked* me, Jackson," I burst out. "It was my first time. Did you know that?"

Jackson blinks at me, green eyes wide. "No. No, baby, I didn't know that. I should have been different. I should have made it special."

"It *was* special," I insist. "It was special until you started talking about her."

"I know this isn't an excuse, but I was drunk—" he starts, and I cut him off, holding up a hand.

"Are you drunk now? Because I'm not listening to anything you say if you're drunk."

"I'm not! I swear. You can ask the guys, I haven't had a drop. Someone spilled a beer on me when I went to the bar to get a soda, Zo, I promise you."

I stare at him but his eyes seem clear.

"I'm sorry that I was a mess back then. I'm sorry that I was a dumbass. But I'm sober now, and I want to make things right."

"What about all the perfume I smell on you?" I accuse, unable to help myself. I'm the jealous type and he does smell something like roses and musk as well as beer.

"Just fans. Locke wanted to take pictures to rile up Gemma," he pleads. "I swear, I didn't talk to any other girls. I was just getting advice from the guys."

"Advice about what?" I ask warily.

"You," he says simply, searching my face. "All I ever think about is you, Zoe."

I'm this close to weakening, to throwing myself in his arms, but I keep stiff, watching him. But there's something else bothering me. There's something else that's been bothering me since I began helping him record the backup vocals for the two songs for his solo album. I'd heard him perform *Red* on stage at the concert I went to, and his voice had been raw and filled with emotion. It was like I went back there all over again, how devastated he'd sounded when he told me that she was gone.

"What about the song?" I demand to know.

"What song?" he asks, frowning.

"*Red*," I explain. "The one about Maria. You always sing it with so much emotion. Are you even over her, after all these years?"

"Yes," he assures me, and he sounds genuine. "Yes, I'm over Maria and I have been for years. I only want you, Zoe."

"Then why do you sing it like that?" I ask, not convinced, trembling because I'm so mad that he's remembered, feeling the way I felt then all over again.

Jackson runs a hand through his long hair. "It was the heartbreak of my life, Zoe. Can't you understand that?"

It's an arrow through my heart, those words, and I look away from him before the tears begin to fall.

"Yeah, I get it, Jackson. Because you were mine."

He stares at me, takes another step forward to put his hand on my cheek.

"I'm so sorry, Zoe. Baby blue. Could you ever forgive me?"

I look into his green eyes, tears streaming down my cheeks, and push him away, overwhelmed. He stumbles backward and I use that time to get into the tour bus, locking the door.

Jackson knocks on the window, calling my name, but I just put my head in my hands, sobbing.

I don't know if I can forgive him. All this time, I've been living some kind of teenage dream of mine, hooking up with the love of my life and not thinking about the consequences. I have been pushing away the heartbreak, the way he'd hurt me so much all those years ago. I have been pushing away the inevitability of him finding out that Elijah is his, too.

Everything seems like too much, all of a sudden, and I can't talk to him. I can't look at him. I don't know why it hurts so much but I guess it's because I've been avoiding it, blocking it out. I'd had the greatest night of my life and he'd woken up gasping and sobbing, nearly throwing up because he was so upset... about someone else. After he'd taken my virginity, after he'd told me how beautiful I was.

I guess I haven't forgiven him yet, but it's not fair, because he doesn't even know that he's the father of my son. It's not fair of me to hate him for a heartbreak from four years ago, but I can't help it.

I want to be his, but I don't want any obstacles, and the way that he sang *Red*, the way he'd told me it was his first heartbreak–it hurts me. I don't know what to do, so I stay in the tour bus, ignoring his cries.

I can't deal with this right now.

Chapter 17

Jackson

I rush back into The Dirty Dozen, looking for Gemma, who has my best friend's tongue halfway down her throat. I guess they'd made up quickly.

I grab her by the shoulder.

"I need the keys to the tour bus."

She glares at me. "What? Why?"

I sigh heavily. "It's a long story."

"A long story? That's funny, I've got plenty of time, I just ordered a burger," Gemma chirps, sitting down at the table and I shift my weight from foot to foot, antsy.

"Gemma, please," I say, and Locke gives me a look.

"Spill," he says, and Gemma props her chin in her hand, looking at me intently.

"I'm seeing Zoe," I mumble, and Gemma's eyes widen.

"Oh, you mean you remember that you hooked up with her?" she asks, and I blink at her.

"What? No! I mean, yes, but I mean I'm seeing her *now*."

Gemma gapes at me. "*What*? You're seeing my best friend?" she screeches.

111

I wince. "Yes, yes, but again, you have literally no right to talk about that," I say, pointing directly at Locke.

Gemma frowns. "I guess not, but still, you could have told me. I can't believe you didn't tell me that you hooked up before."

"I didn't remember that until recently," I say honestly. "But I've been seeing her since the last tour, off and on. I just didn't know it was the same girl."

Gemma looks at me like I'm the stupidest person she's ever seen, and I have to admit I deserve it. "Really, Jackson?"

"Really, Gemma," I say dryly. "And now she's mad at me and she locked herself in the tour bus and I *really* need to talk to her."

"What's she mad at you about?" Gemma drawls. "Is it the fact that you totally forgot that you took her virginity?"

I tighten my jaw and Axel gapes at me as if he hadn't thought of that conclusion.

"That, and... something else."

"Guess you better tell me if you want those keys."

"I can't stand you," I say through gritted teeth, but my annoying little sister just grins up at me. "Back then, I was still fucked up about Maria, and I guess I talked to her about it... after."

"After you *slept* with her?" she asks, her eyes widening.

"Yes," I sigh, and Gemma shakes her head.

"No way. There is *no way* I'm giving you the keys now. You totally deserve to be locked out."

"How am I supposed to make it up to her if I can't even talk to her?" I ask, exasperated.

Gemma shrugs. "Guess you'll have to figure that out some other day."

She waves to the server. "Can I get that burger to go?"

"Gemma," I plead, but she's not having it. My little sister can be as stubborn as a bull when she wants to be.

"Absolutely not, Jackson. She needs some space to think, and you're going to give it to her. That's the least you can do right now."

"She thinks I'm still not over Maria!" I protest. "That's ridiculous, I've been over her for years."

"Yet, you wrote a song about her," Gemma drawls.

"How did you know it was about her?"

"Who *else* would it be about?" She stares at me as if it should be obvious.

Axel nods. "Yeah, it is pretty obvious, man."

"Traitor," I mumble.

Locke is pouting in Gemma's direction. "Can I come home with you?"

Gemma narrows her eyes at him. "Are you done flirting with fans?"

"Yes," he says sheepishly, smiling, and she stares a bit longer.

"Nope," she finally chirps, and Locke groans.

"Why not?"

"Because I'm having a girl's day with Zoe, obviously. We're going to go and get our nails done and talk about why men are shit."

"I'm not shit," Locke complains.

"You have been before," she says easily. "So, I'll have plenty to talk about. You guys have fun the rest of the night. Don't forget to pick up Cain in the morning."

"As if I'd forget to pick up our son," Locke scoffs, but Gemma doesn't seem to care that he's grumpy.

She walks out and I look after her, wondering if I could go outside and try to talk to Zoe again. Maybe Gemma is right. Maybe I need to give her some time.

"You know, used to be we'd order a round of tequila shots and stay out all night, go to after-parties," Axel says, a little glumly. "Now we're just sitting here getting fat and talking about women."

"We could rehearse," Locke says.

"It's almost midnight," I say. "Where the hell are we going to rehearse?"

"Your place? You're the single one," Axel says.

"Don't remind me," I mumble, but I agree and we split up, Axel and Locke to go and get their supplies and me to drive home and open up the garage.

It has the best acoustics, after all, even though my neighbors will *definitely* complain about us practicing so late at night. Our next show in Dallas is in less than a week, though, so we definitely need to start rehearsing anyway.

Axel and Locke show up after a few moments and then Samuel shows up too, driving his brand-new car. I glare at him a little, but I guess it's not his fault that he and Zoe have become friends.

"What's going on?" Samuel asks, and Locke claps him on the back.

"Jackson's having a crisis," he says.

"A total crisis," Axel responds. "He's in love with the stylist."

"No one said I was in love," I protest, although I've been thinking that for the past few weeks, if I'm honest with myself.

Samuel's eyes widen. "Oh, Zoe? Wow, I would have never thought."

"Why's that?" I snap, and Samuel shrugs.

"I dunno. I didn't know you were her type."

I take a couple of steps toward him. "What, and you are?"

Axel puts a hand on my chest. "Calm down, tiger. Samuel's got a girlfriend, remember?"

As far as I know, it's not serious, so I don't know how far that goes. I grumble but set up the microphone anyway.

"We've got to stop opening with *Keyed Up*," Axel complains. "I feel like everyone's getting tired of it."

"Hey!" Locke protests defensively. "People love *Keyed Up*."

"I still think *Amped Up* is better," Axel brags.

"Yeah, yeah, your one song about partying and heartbreak," I drawl, poking fun at Axel since he's only penned one of our many songs.

"Your songs are literally all about breakups, shut up," Axel mutters.

I want to tell him that one of them isn't about a breakup, but no one has heard the lyrics to *Blue* yet, so I'm not sure I want to let them hear it yet.

Samuel looks around as if confused. "Why is Jackson bucking up at me about Zoe?"

"He thinks you guys are flirty," Locke says idly, setting up his drum set.

"*What*? I really do have a girlfriend," Samuel complains.

"We haven't met her," I complain. "So she could be imaginary for all we know."

"I've met her," Axel pipes in. "She kinda used to be my landlord."

I blink. "That's a weird story."

Samuel flushes. "I don't know why we're suddenly talking about my love life."

"Just trying to keep Jackson from clocking you for being friends with his girl," Axel tells him, and I make a harrumph sound in the back of my throat.

"I wasn't going to hit him," I mumble, but I'm still in a

115

bad mood. It's not like I actually think Samuel has his sights on Zoe. I know he's not like that, and he's not a flirty person in general, but it seems like they have a bit of a connection. They're always talking when she comes to give us our new clothes and he's just chattier than normal with her, that's all.

"Seriously, Jack, I didn't know you were seeing her. We're really just friends," Samuel says earnestly, and I feel kind of bad for hating him a little.

"Yeah, okay," I say, and give him a smile. He gives me a wan smile back.

Samuel takes off his tie and takes his position on the other side of the microphone and I tap it to get started.

"One, two, three, let's go!"

Chapter 18

Zoe

I'm still crying when Gemma comes out to the tour bus, and she puts a hand on my shoulder.

"I'm sorry that my brother was such a douche to you all those years ago," she says comfortingly, and I sniffle.

"It isn't your fault."

"I know, but it's *your* fault that you didn't tell me," she chides, cranking up the bus and pulling out slowly, avoiding the parked cars behind us. I bite at the cuticle of my thumb, not knowing how to answer that at first.

"I was just so hurt," I finally say. "I was so hurt and then I found out I was pregnant and I felt so alone."

"You wouldn't have been alone, Zoe. I would have been your best friend and we could have gotten through it," Gemma insists.

"Maybe," I murmur. "I guess I was afraid you'd take his side or something. You guys were always really close."

Gemma frowns. "I guess I can understand that." She takes in a deep breath. "I've always been the one to love Jackson unconditionally and let him get away with anything. I don't think I would have let him get away with hurting you, though."

"I should have told you. I should have told *someone*, pregnancy was awfully lonely."

"I can't imagine," Gemma says softly. "Harley was the same way, she ghosted us when she got pregnant and did it all by herself up until Jazz was born. I folded and told Axel almost right away, and then Locke found out before I was even eight weeks along."

I laugh. "You've never been one to keep secrets."

"I almost did, from Locke anyway. He didn't act nearly as whipped as he does now. I didn't even know if he liked me, or just liked fucking me. You know how that goes."

"Oh, do I," I say darkly. That's exactly the problem I have with Jackson, or at least the problem I used to have. I guess that now at least I know he might want to actually date me, but once he knows the truth, it'll be a whole different situation.

"I didn't tell him, by the way," Gemma tells me, and I go a little pale.

I haven't even considered that she might go ahead and tell him, in a heated argument or something. Thank God my best friend is good at keeping other people's secrets even if she isn't at keeping her own.

"Thank you," I say gratefully, and I mean it. My head is beginning to hurt, probably from the cheap wine I've been drinking at Gemma's. "Do you think you could take me home?"

Gemma pouts. "I thought we could have a girl's night, but I'll take you home on one condition."

"What's that?" I ask, looking at her sideways."

She grins. "You let me meet my nephew."

Two hours later, Gemma's on the floor building some

Lego atrocity with Elijah. It isn't going to stand up for very long, but when Elijah giggles and cheers when it falls over, I realize they're playing some kind of version of Lego Jenga.

"You're not much of an architect, kiddo," I tell him, ruffling his hair. He seems a lot better, not complaining of his tummy hurting, so I don't feel bad about Gemma being here and potentially passing it on to little Cain.

"I have a little boy, lots younger than you. Do you think you could teach him about Legos?" Gemma asks, and Elijah lights up.

"Another kid? I love other kids," he says, like he hasn't socialized a day in his life.

I roll my eyes. "You meet lots of other kids at daycare, honey."

"Not babies," he complains. "Never babies, and babies always smell nice."

"They do," Gemma agrees, smiling and looking at him fondly. "Their heads always smell so sweet, don't they?"

Elijah nods. "When can I meet him?"

"Soon," I say softly, and give Gemma a look.

Gemma lets Elijah start building again and comes over to talk to me in the hallway.

"I don't know about playdates. Not yet," I tell her, and Gemma frowns.

"You don't have long before you need to tell him, Zoe. It's only a few weeks before the tour is over and I promise you, if you don't tell him, I will."

"I'm going to tell him after the Albuquerque show," I promise.

Gemma looks at me for a long moment. "You better," she says finally.

All I can do until then is avoid Jackson as long as I can.

* * *

After double checking with my mom that it's okay to leave Elijah with her for two days while I fly out to Dallas to style the guys, I get busy shopping. I do most of my shopping back home, but I pick up a few pieces in Dallas, including a black cowboy hat for Locke that Gemma is enamored with.

I get lucky dropping off Jackson's things, because he's not at the hotel room and I end up just giving them to Gemma.

She frowns at me a little. "You're not avoiding him, are you?"

"A little," I admit. "But I'm still mad at him."

Gemma nods. "Okay, that's fair. I'll take them to him when he gets in, he went to grab us all some lunch."

I give her Locke's clothes too and she deposits everything back in her room before I go to drop off Axel's stuff.

There's a baby screaming in his hotel room and I raise an eyebrow when he opens the door.

Axel grins. "Had to bring my girls with me," he says, and I smile a little, dropping off his clothes.

Samuel's next, and he's on the same floor as Jackson so I go back up the elevator, standing at the door of his room for a long moment.

He finally comes to the door, looking exhausted and with his hair all over the place.

"You good?" I ask, and he nods tiredly.

"Just exhausted. Was up late last night," he says, and takes the clothes from me, throwing them on the bed. I wince a little, thinking those are freshly pressed, but I don't complain.

They're rockstars, after all, not businessmen.

I take a step inside, biting at my cuticle. "Can I ask you something?"

"Sure." He smiles.

I don't close the door, just take another step inside for privacy.

"I've kind of got a dilemma going on, and I'm not sure what to do."

"Shoot," he says easily, sitting down on the edge of the bed.

"I've got this guy, and we kind of have a past."

"Uh-huh," Samuel nods, smiling just slightly.

"And he broke my heart, but now he wants to date me."

Samuel raises an eyebrow. "Is it your son's father?" he asks, and I blink at him.

Samuel is astute, and I wonder if he's put it together already. Even if he has, I'm not going to confirm it for him.

"Yes," I finally admit, and Samuel spreads his hands as if the answer is obvious.

"Then sure, I think you should go for it. Everyone makes mistakes, Zoe. But you could have your family back together."

I think about it for a moment, how Jackson and Elijah had both crossed their legs at the same time, how Elijah had fallen asleep curled up next to his father.

"I don't know if he wants a family," I say softly, and Samuel looks up at me.

"You can't know if you don't ask, Zoe," he reminds me gently, and he's right.

I can't know what Jackson wants until I talk to him, until I tell him the truth, but I'm just not ready to do that now. I might be angry with him about what happened all those years ago, but once I tell him, he will absolutely hate me for lying to him.

I take in a deep breath.

"Thank you," I tell him gratefully. "That helps a lot, even if I might not take your advice."

Samuel smiles wryly. "No one ever does."

He walks me to the door, shutting it behind me, and I make my way to the elevator, feeling just a little bit lighter. Telling the truth has it's upsides, it turns out, and I'm pretty sure Samuel knows what I'm talking about even if I didn't actually confirm it.

Secrets can eat you alive.

Chapter 19

Jackson

I'm holding five boxes of pizza and trying to balance them against the door while searching for the hotel key in my pocket when I hear a familiar voice.

"Can I ask you something?"

Samuel's room is just a couple down from mine and I instantly put the pizza on the floor, walking closer. I pray that no one shuts the door, and my prayers are answered. I know that the right thing to do would be not to listen in on their conversation, but Zoe won't answer my texts or calls, and I miss her.

I miss her, and I don't know what she's feeling so I tell myself this is the only way to find out. It's not like Gemma's going to spill. She's close-mouthed about her best friend's secrets.

"And he broke my heart, and now he wants to date me."

I wince. I hate thinking that I broke Zoe's heart, but then Samuel asks the question, the one I've been thinking all this time.

"Is it's your son's father?"

My heart drops to my toes when she says yes, and when

Samuel gives her the advice to keep her family together, I could have run in there and throttled him.

The guy obviously broke her heart, and as far as I know, he has no contact with Elijah. I've never seen him around, any of this time that I'd been spending with her. So he gets to go ghost and break her heart and she's supposed to what, get back together with him?

I don't know for sure that it's him, but something nags at me about the guy who'd been at her house, the one with the salt and pepper hair. He was so much *older* than her. What a creep. I ignore the fact that I had hooked up with her when she was young and am also quite a bit older than her. He's a shitty dad and I bet he's an even shittier boyfriend.

I feel dejected as I finally get into the hotel room with the pizzas and I wish I could eat them until I make myself sick instead of calling everyone else to my room. Something washes over me, some kind of competitive nature, and I realize that I don't want to give up. I'm not going to let this asshole take my girl, no matter what kind of history they have.

I'll get Zoe fair and square, or fight dirty. I don't care, I have no respect for the man who left her and a baby in the lurch years ago.

When I call everyone over for pizza, I hope that Zoe comes. She's part of the group text now, after all, but she never shows and my shoulders slump. I still feel a little dejected about what she'd said to Samuel, and I keep glaring at him. He knows I'm seeing her, for God's sake, so why would he give her that kind of advice?

Samuel ignores me, happily chomping on four slices of pizza before excusing himself to go back to bed.

Axel takes a few slices for himself and Harley and goes back to the room.

"Sorry to split, but Jazz has been a holy terror ever since the plane. Turns out she doesn't like traveling nearly as much as her dad," he apologizes.

Gemma nods, understanding. They'd left Cain at home with an overnight sitter for two days, an older woman named Ella who was kind and wonderful with kids. She keeps telling Axel and Harley to use her but Axel just can't let Jazz stay anywhere that isn't with him and Harley. He's overly attached, Locke says, but Gemma thinks it's sweet.

"I'm going to do something big to make it up to Zoe," I say, and Gemma looks at me curiously.

"How big?"

"I'm going to perform a song I wrote for her."

Gemma's eyes widen. "Oh my God, you wrote a song for her?" She smacks Locke on the shoulder. "How come you never write songs for me?"

"I only had one in me," Locke complained with a mouthful of pizza, the one with pineapple on it that only he and Gemma liked. Monsters.

"I don't want to give away the surprise, so don't say anything," I warn Gemma, and she makes a zipping motion across her lips.

"Not a word," she promises.

"Tell Samuel to come to my room," I say mysteriously, and Gemma cocks her head at me but she doesn't ask questions.

When she and Locke leave, it's only a few moments before Samuel comes over, dragging his feet.

I glare at him but he doesn't seem to notice. As mad as I am at him, I feel bad for the poor guy, he looks more than exhausted.

"I want you to sing lead vocals for the last three songs," I tell him, and Samuel just stares at me like I've grown two heads.

"*Me?*" he asks incredulously.

"Yes, you. You've got the right voice for the last songs, and I've got plans. I'm also going to perform a new song I wrote, right after *Amped Up*. Tell the other guys, okay?"

"I mean... okay, I guess. Is this just for this show?"

"I hope so," I say firmly. I hope that it doesn't take two or three grand gestures to get Zoe to date me.

"All right," he agrees tiredly. "Just don't wake me up until rehearsal."

"Noted."

He doesn't seem to notice that I'm cold to him, but I guess it doesn't matter. If Zoe says yes, then I'll forgive him.

* * *

I frown, looking around for Zoe as the opening bars of *Amped Up* begin. I don't see her right away, and then finally I catch sight of her shock of blue hair in the middle of the crowd. She isn't up front like Gemma, but she's watching, swaying along to the music, and I guess that's a good sign. I try to catch her eye but she's watching Locke do his drum solo, and I guess that's okay.

After *Amped Up* is over, I'm sweating. It's a hard rock song, and there's a lot of raspy parts, so I clear my throat a few times, drinking from my bottle of water on stage. Once upon a time that would have been a beer, but I'm staying away from booze, especially when I feel so out of control.

"We're going to do something a little different tonight," I announce, and the crowd roars and cheers. There's a few girls trying to jump over the barricade, but the bouncers at the bar are keeping them at bay. We're pretty popular in Dallas, so sometimes, the crowd can get rowdy.

"I've got a song I've been working on for someone pretty special," I continue. "It's called *Baby Blue*."

I change the name at the very last second, just so she'll be sure it's for her, and she freezes in the middle of the crowd but she doesn't run away, so I think that's a good sign.

"*My baby's blue,*" it starts, and the crowd loses it, loving the ballad style. We don't have many of those, and I guess they really like it. The song goes on to explain that blue has become my favorite color and that with my baby blue, I'll never be blue again. The background vocals, which I've tuned up in the background, are Zoe's harmonizing, and the crowd loves it just as much as I do.

Zoe doesn't dance along to the music, just watches me on stage, biting one of her cuticles, and finally I jump down over the barricade. Fans are all over me and I high five a few of them, grab some hands to shake, but I'm only looking at Zoe.

She watches me approach her, her blue eyes wide, and I speak into the microphone.

"Will you be mine, baby blue?"

Zoe gasps and she looks at me for a long moment before she pushes through the crowd, running outside.

Well, shit. That isn't what I anticipated happening, but the crowd seems to love the drama, so I run back on stage and hand Samuel the microphone.

"D-don't worry, guys, Jack will be back," he stutters, but I don't plan on coming back tonight. I sprint outside, looking for Zoe.

I find her out back, taking deep breaths.

"God, I wish I still smoked," she gasps.

"Are you okay?" I ask her, and when she nods, I get closer to her.

"Was that a no?"

Zoe shakes her head and I frown.

"I mean," she starts, and then takes a deep breath. "I just didn't expect that much attention, Jackson. There was a spotlight and everything."

I laugh a little, relieved. "I'm sorry, baby blue. I thought it would be one of those, you know, grand gestures. To show you how much I..." I trail off, not sure if I want to use that word yet, the "I love you." It's a big moment for me, and I don't want it to be too soon, even if I feel it.

"I don't know if I can give you an answer yet," she hedges.

I frown. "Why not? I want you to be my girlfriend, Zoe, if that wasn't obvious."

"I don't know if that's what you really want," she says in a small voice.

"That's what I really want!" I burst out. "It's what I've wanted ever since I saw you in Albuquerque."

"I've wanted you a lot longer than that," she says with a wry smile.

"Gemma knows," I warn her, and she pales just slightly.

"Knows what?"

"Knows that we've been dating."

"How did she take it?" she asks, looking away from me, and I wonder if she had already told her because she doesn't seem a bit surprised.

"She doesn't care," I say flippantly. "Although she'll probably give me attitude about it for about a year."

"So that means all the obstacles are over, huh?" she asks quietly.

I take her chin in my hand, forcing her to look at me. "I think so. Except for one."

Her eyes shoot to mine. "What's that?"

"Don't choose him."

"Choose who?" she asks, looking baffled, and my jaw tightens.

"I heard you talking to Samuel," I say tightly. "I heard you say that your ex wants you back. I even met the fucker when I went to see you and he answered the door."

Zoe's mouth drops open. "You... you *met* him?"

"Yeah." I take a couple steps back, taking in deep breaths through my nostrils. "You didn't tell me he was back in the picture." I feel angry about that, suddenly, and I don't want to show it, so I look away.

"You met *Dexter,*" she says, like that's supposed to mean something to me.

I snort. "That's a terrible name. Glad you didn't name the kid after him."

"I never would," she continues, taking a step toward me. This time she's the one who takes my chin in her hand, turning me to look at her. "He's not the father, you idiot."

"Then why was some guy answering your door?" I pout.

"He's my older sister's boyfriend," she says with a laugh. "They were staying with me for a few days."

Relief floods over me. "Oh, thank God. He was way too old for you, anyway."

"You're not much younger than him," Zoe teases, and I scoff.

"I'm better looking," I say, running a hand through my hair, and she gives me this half smile.

"Definitely," she agrees, and kisses my chin, my cheek, my other cheek, before pressing her lips against mine.

"Is this a yes?" I ask against her mouth, refusing to open my lips, and she giggles.

"It's a yes," she says, and I forget all about her conversation with Samuel and why I should still be worried.

I kiss her hard, pressing her up against the brick, shoving my hands down the legging that she's wearing to part the triangle of pubic hair on her slit, pressing my fingers against her clit.

She moans into my mouth, finally sticking her tongue inside, and her mouth is as hot as her sex. She rolls her hips against my hand wantonly.

"We should go back to your room," she gasps, and I grin.

"Don't have to sneak you in, not this time," I murmur, slowly removing my hand from her pants. I pop my fingers into my mouth to suck her juices off and she groans loudly.

"You're such a demon when you do that," she mumbles, and I grin at her.

"You like it," I accuse, and she rolls her eyes but she's smiling.

"It's fucking hot," she agrees, and I take her hand. "Shouldn't you finish your set?"

I shake my head. "Samuel can deal with the rest. I want to take you to my room and ravish you."

"Ravish? Where'd you get that, a Harlequin romance?" she teases.

I can't stop smiling. I like her so much. I'm falling in love with her, and I have been since I first saw her again at that first concert we met up at. I keep telling myself it's too soon to tell her that, too soon to tell her that I'm head over heels, but the words stick in my throat, wanting to come out.

The hotel is within walking distance, about a quarter of a mile, and I keep hold of her hand tight as we walk.

"How's Elijah doing?" I ask, and she looks startled just for a moment.

"He's on the mend," she says. "He was a little mad at me for coming to a concert without him, but I think he's a little too young."

I laugh. "He'd love a concert. He loves loud music."

Zoe gives me a small smile. "He does."

"Takes after his father, you said," I mumble, remembering. I don't know why it bothers me so much, that her ex is also a musician, but somehow it does.

Zoe goes a little pale and I squeeze her hand. She shakes her head a little.

"That last drink packed a punch, I guess," she mutters.

"I could carry you the rest of the way," I suggest. "Piggy back?"

Zoe smiles and I turn so that she can hop on my back, holding her by her thick thighs.

I can't wait to get her back to the hotel, but I wouldn't mind if we just talked and held each other all night. Once upon a time, I'd be taking multiple women to bed, focused only on the sex, but things are different with Zoe.

God, I'm definitely not the rockstar I once was.

Chapter 20

Zoe

Maybe it's a bad idea to give into Jackson's advances for dating. In fact, I'm *sure* it's a bad idea. The more time I spend with him, the more I'm going to fall, and then eventually, I'm going to have to tell him that Elijah is his.

I suppose that I've always had an issue with wanting to give people a second chance, and Jackson really seems like he's changed. I had thought that about my father, too, though, and look how that had turned out.

I bite at the cuticle of my thumb, tearing it so that it bleeds as Jackson uses the key to open the hotel door.

Jackson tsks when he notices it. "Oh, baby blue," he mourns. "You're bleeding."

"Bad habit," I admit, and Jackson takes me to the bathroom, running my thumb under the water. When it begins to run clear he pops my thumb into his mouth, sucking gently.

I gasp, a shiver running down my spine as he removes it from his mouth and smiles at me.

My body is vibrating and all I want is to jump into his arms and tear his clothes off.

Jackson leans down to kiss me and I moan into his mouth, doing exactly like I want and jumping up into his arms. He catches me with a laugh into my mouth, stumbling backward and taking me over to the bed, covering my body with his own. He takes his shirt off with one hand between kisses, ripping it off and throwing it onto the floor.

I run my hands up his abs to his chest, digging my nails into his pecs and Jackson growls deep in his throat.

"I love it when you do that," he murmurs. "Love when you mark me up with those nails."

Fuck. It's like everything that Jackson says and does either makes me hot or makes my heart ache, and I have no idea how I'm going to start dating him without losing my mind.

Jackson's hard against my thigh and I reach between us to grab him through his tailored jeans.

"These jeans basically had to be sewed on," he groans, thrusting into my hand, and I help him unbutton them and push them down his ass, freeing his cock which stands long and pretty against his stomach.

I don't have anything to compare it to, not exactly. Jackson doesn't have the only penis I've ever seen, but it's the only one I've ever had inside me, and it fits perfectly. We're like puzzle pieces. When we first hooked up, I told myself it was because we were meant to be together. I can't deny that some part of me still believes that our bodies fit together because we fit together all other ways, too.

My head is spinning. I don't know why I've agreed to this and part of me wants to backtrack, tell Jackson that we can't date, but this is all I've ever wanted. My whole life, I have wanted Jackson Arden, and now he wants me, too.

Jackson lines up, hefting my legs up and hooking my knees over his biceps, and I roll my hips up to give him better access, spreading my thighs further. He thrusts into me, not gently. He's pent up, it seems, and that's okay, because I am too.

As soon as he enters me my inner muscles clench around him and he leans down to kiss me, pressing my thighs up, nearly putting my ankles on the headboard.

My muscles ache but in a good way, like after a good workout, and I moan into his mouth as he hits just the right spot. Jackson knows exactly what I like, even though we've only been hooking up for a few months. He knows exactly where to touch me, exactly what strokes to use, and again, that part of my brain that thinks we might be meant to be lights up.

What if Jackson's the one? I've always believed that there is a person out there for everyone, that when you're born, your counterpart is selected for you. My mother always told me that. She always said that my father was her soulmate, and you don't give up on your soulmate. That turned out to be hard for her, but she eventually did have to give up.

I worry that's what will happen to me, that Jackson will hate me when I tell him that Elijah is his, or worse, he won't and he and I will be together and he'll go back to his old ways. Jackson may not be an addict like my father, but he definitely uses partying as a crutch, or at least he used to. He did when I met him, when Maria broke up with him, and I'd heard around town that he fell into a bottle when things got rough.

Jackson might have that gene inside him, that switch that gets flipped, the same one that my father has. I'm terrified, but I can't think about it right now. I can't think about anything right now but how Jackson feels inside me, how he's stretching me out.

I drag my nails down his shoulders and he hisses.

"I love the way they sting in the shower later," he murmurs, fucking me faster, breathing hard. "Reminds me of you."

He always knows just what to say, just how to move to tip me over the edge and I'm coming, stars exploding behind my closed lids. When I open my eyes, Jackson's focused on how he's pumping in and out of me, holding my legs apart and I whimper, thinking that I might come twice before he gets done.

He seems focused but it's only a few moments before his thrusts begin to lose rhythm and I know he's close.

"Fill me up," I say throatily, and Jackson groans as he comes inside me. I feel him pulsing and I sigh happily, feeling warm all over and sated.

Jackson slowly pulls out of me, lying beside me and putting his hands behind his head, panting as he looks up at the ceiling. I take the opportunity to lie my head on his chest, listen to his heartbeat. He puts one arm around me. He's definitely a cuddler after sex, and I wonder if he's like that with everybody. I scrunch up my nose, thinking that I definitely don't want to know.

"Zoe?" Jackson calls, and I look up at him, smiling.

"Hmm?"

"What are you thinking about?" He's frowning slightly.

I tilt my head. "Isn't that a question mostly women ask?"

He barks out a laugh. "Maybe, but I still want to know. Penny for your thoughts, and all that."

"I wasn't really thinking anything," I admit. "Just about how you're kind of a cuddler after sex. I was sort of wondering if you were like that with everyone."

Jackson grins. "And if I am?"

I scrunch my nose again. "I wouldn't like it."

"I'm not," he admits. "Before you, it was mostly flings. There was only one girl I got serious about between Maria and you."

I prop myself up on my elbow. "Really? You're a rock-star, you must have had lots of girls who wanted to date you."

"I wasn't in the right place to date anyone," he confesses. "I was a mess after Maria, for a really long time. I'm not good with breakups."

"I remember," I say sourly.

Jackson sits up straighter, putting his back against the headboard. I admire his looks, his long torso, his broad shoulders. He's lanky, not as broad as some of the other members of the Spades, but just my type, defined abs with a smaller chest than Axel.

"What I did to you was really shitty, Zoe, and I'm sorry," he says earnestly.

"It was shitty," I agree. "But the sex wasn't." I try to lighten the mood, not wanting him to feel guilty.

Jackson's frown deepens. He takes my hand, brings my knuckles to his lips to kiss them.

"Seriously, baby blue. I should have never hooked up with you knowing that I wasn't over Maria. God, you were so young—"

I put one finger over his lips. "I was grown enough," I tell him. "I was a couple of months away from turning eighteen, and I wanted you. You didn't take my virginity, I gave it to you."

"I had no idea you were a virgin, either," Jackson groans, ignoring me trying to shush him. "I don't even remember it, Zoe, and I'm so sorry."

"You were gentle," I say softly. It still stings that he barely remembers it, only enough to finally realize that it happened, but I suppose I should have known. He was more than three sheets to the wind that night, and I'd known that.

"Yeah?" he asks hopefully, tilting his head to nuzzle against my neck. "I was okay?"

"It was wonderful," I admit. "Until you started crying about your ex."

Jackson covers his face with his hands and peeks out at me from between his fingers.

"That's so terrible, baby blue, I'm an idiot."

"You were," I say dryly. "Hopefully, not anymore."

He shakes his head empathically. "Not anymore. At least, I'm trying."

He shifts back down on the bed, drawing me into his arms.

"Zoe?" he calls again, and I turn to look at him. "You're not still talking to the baby's father, right?"

I frown, unsure how to answer that. "From time to time," I hedge, so that it isn't a complete and utter lie. I'm a bad liar, and I know he'll see right through me if I say no outright.

Jackson pouts and it's cute and I can't help but kiss him, giggling a little.

"It's not like that," I promise him. "I'm not dating him." *That* was a lie, or at least it would be, if I continued dating Jackson. I can't very well tell him that I'm dating the father of my child without revealing everything, though.

He draws me closer, kissing along my neck. "Good. I don't want you to see anyone else. We're exclusive now."

"We are?" I murmur. "Already?"

"Yes, already. I want you all to myself," Jackson says, biting down on the base of my neck and making me moan.

"Want me to be all yours?" I ask, loving it when he's possessive. It just means he wants me, that he wants only me and he doesn't want anyone else to touch me, and there's something about it that makes me shiver with pleasure.

"All mine," Jackson growls, biting me again, leaving a mark by sucking there, and I arch my body against his. I straddle his lap, rocking my hips against him and he slides into me easily, having not adjusted himself back into his jeans.

"I'm all yours, Jackson," I moan, and Jackson thrusts up beneath me, taking hold of my hips, leaving fingerprint bruises that I could marvel at days later.

Jackson Arden wants me. It's all I've ever wanted, and now it's happening.

"Fuck," Jackson curses, and before I'm able to climax he comes inside me, and he groans. "Sorry. I just love it when you say that," he apologizes.

I giggle. Sex for me isn't always about the orgasm, and I know he'll make up for it. He's good with his fingers and his mouth and he never leaves me wanting.

As he trails down my body, kissing my stomach, my hip bones, my inner thighs, I wonder how I got so lucky and so unlucky at the same time.

Jackson Arden wants me. But he doesn't know that I had his child four years ago. And when I have to tell him, that can ruin everything.

Chapter 21

Jackson

Everything is perfect. I'm watching Zoe sleep in my arms, the way her eyelids flutter, the way her mouth is slightly open, and even her soft snore is cute to me.

Damnit. I'm in love with her, and I don't know how to tell her. She seems wary for so many reasons, the biggest one being that I broke her heart all those years ago. I can't imagine how it must have felt for me to have taken her virginity and then have a breakdown about Maria.

I keep trying to remember exactly what happened, but all I can remember is kissing her and then her rubbing my back as I talked about Maria. It makes me cringe, and it's not the best first memory with the woman I love.

I *do* love her, and if I tell her that, she might run, so what I have to focus on now is making her believe it. I have to be a good guy for her. I have to be the *right* guy for her, and I need to show her.

She wakes slowly, blinking those gorgeous blue eyes, and I smile at her. She smiles back, rubbing at her face.

"Is it too late for breakfast?"

I look at my phone. "Not if we hurry, ends in thirty minutes."

Zoe hops out of bed, going to the bathroom to wash her face and brush her teeth, and I groan as I tug off the tightest jeans in the world that Zoe had styled me in, having slept in them.

There are literal marks on my thighs from how tight they are and Zoe giggles at them when she comes out of the bathroom, dressed in one of my T-shirts and a pair of yoga pants, the ones I love to see the curve of her ass in.

"Maybe those were a little too tight," she says.

"You think?" I ask incredulously, and she bursts into giggles again. I can't help but laugh with her, she's so bright and bubbly when she wants to be, and I love that about her.

"I love everything about you," I want to say, but I don't.

"I love your laugh," is what I end up with, and Zoe's bright smile makes it worth it.

"I think I kind of sound like a hyena," she says with another giggle.

"Maybe a little," I tease, and she pushes me with one hand. I dramatically fall on the bed, and she jumps on top of me.

"Maybe we don't need breakfast," she murmurs, but then her stomach protests, growling loudly.

"I think we do," I insist, laughing softly. She pouts but stands up, letting me finish getting dressed in a pair of sweats and a Van Halen t-shirt.

When we make it down for breakfast, Gemma cheers when she sees us and the guys follow suit, even Samuel. I guess he's changed his mind about the advice he gave Zoe about dating Elijah's father, so I can forgive him.

I grin and Zoe blushes.

"I hope there's not a rule against fraternization," Zoe says playfully, and Gemma snorts.

"Don't worry, babe, I'm the only thing we have for human resources and I'm married to the drummer. You're all good."

Locke laughs and puts his arm around her.

"I'm just a groupie," Harley chirps, and Axel bursts out laughing.

"The prettiest groupie ever," Axel coos and kisses her, and Samuel rolls his eyes.

"You guys know how to make someone feel painfully single."

"Thought you had a girl?" Axel asks, munching on bacon, and Samuel shrugs.

"I do, it's just kind of on and off," he admits in a mumble, and everyone notices his mood change so we collectively drop it.

We've been a band long enough to know when one of us wants to talk about something and when we don't, and it's a strange kind of telepathic connection. We've just been friends and a band so long that we understand each other. We're a family, and I think Zoe will fit in just fine.

I want to ride with Zoe on the trip home, but Gemma convinces me to ride in the tour bus.

"You don't want to rush her, Jack," she advises, and she's right.

I can't wait until we get back home, and I can finally take her out on a real date.

* * *

"It's not roller skating," I assure her, and Zoe smiles.

"Roller skating would be fun, right, Elijah?" He's holding tight to her hand, looking up at me with wide eyes.

Elijah's a little shy, and it's been a while since we hung out together in the studio. He was sick then, too, so I guess he gave me a little more leeway then.

He doesn't answer his mother, just looks up at her with a small smile. He's so cute, and he has her smile, and I want to pick him up and carry him into the building, but I figure that might freak him out.

"It didn't go so well last time," I said dryly, and she swung my hand back and forth as we walked to the building.

It was nearing eight in the evening, which is when the event starts, so I'm hurrying and she's trying to keep up.

"We have little legs, slow down," she complains, but she's not looking up at the building sign so at least it'll be a surprise.

The lights have just gone down when we get inside, and she gasps.

"Oh my God, I haven't done this since I was fifteen," she says, looking around.

I grin. "Cosmic bowling was always my favorite. I didn't even know they did it anymore."

"Me either!" She smiles at me. "This is so great, Jackson. I hope they have my size in shoes."

"Why wouldn't they?" I ask, curious.

She looks at me. "Haven't you noticed? I have tiny feet. I'm a size five."

I blink. "I didn't even know they made size fives that weren't for children."

Elijah snorts out a laugh and I crouch down. "Do you wear a bigger size than your mama?"

Elijah shakes his head, grinning. "Not yet."

Zoe snorts and hits me with the heel of her hand.

We manage to find a pair of shoes for her, although I'm pretty sure they're from the children's section. She really *does* have tiny feet, and it's just another quirk that I find adorable. It's ridiculous how many things I already love about her, and it's like my heart is full to bursting.

Keep it together, Jackson, I tell myself. *Don't overwhelm her.*

"You're cute," I say simply, and she smiles brightly at me as I put on my bowling shoes (a respectable size twelve).

Elijah stares down at his shoes, frowning. I guess he doesn't know how to tie them yet. My heart seems to swell even more and I wonder if there's something wrong with me or if this kid is just the cutest kid in the world. Next to my nephew Cain, at least.

I sit down next to him and motion for him to put his legs in my lap, and he does so. I tie the shoes up for him.

"Not too tight?" I ask, and he shakes his head.

"Just right," he chirps, and I can't help the grin that spreads across my face.

I've gotten the gutter ball rails so that Elijah won't have a hard time with gutter balls, but Zoe manages somehow not to hit a single pin her first or second roll.

So, she's not the best bowler. *That's one con,* I tell myself, but is it, really? I keep trying to think of *something I* don't like about her.

The thing about falling in love fast and hard is that it can end just as quickly, and I'm already panicking a little, if I'm honest with myself. Zoe and Elijah already feel like my family, somehow, and I can imagine us together, cuddling on the couch watching movies, Elijah and I rocking out in the garage to his favorite songs, eating family dinner. I'm already planning our lives but what if it all goes wrong?

What if Elijah's father comes back into the picture and Zoe leaves me?

I don't think I can take a heartbreak like that.

"Are you okay?" Zoe is looking at me curiously and I realize that I'm standing there putting a hand over my heart.

I drop my hand, moving it to rub across the back of my neck instead, my face flushing.

"Yeah, I'm good. Just waiting to decimate you at bowling."

Zoe pouts. "You should let me win."

"Never!" Elijah pipes up suddenly, and I'm surprised into a laugh. It's his turn next, and he knocks over three pins, beating his mom.

"My son is a regular Homer Simpson," Zoe says with a giggle, and I love the way her face lights up when she laughs.

I knock down all but one pin on the first roll, and Elijah cheers.

"Bet you can't make that spare," Zoe teases, and I puff my chest up.

"Bet I can."

"What do you want to bet?" she asks.

"A kiss," I tell her, and I feel like I'm a teenager all over again when she blushes and looks away, as if I haven't been inside her, begging for me to go harder, faster.

"Fair enough," she mumbles, sitting next to Elijah and watching. I don't make the spare, missing it by just a couple of centimeters, and I curse loudly.

Elijah gasps. "Mr. Jack that's a bad word," he whispers.

I wince. "I know, bud. Sorry, I'll try to keep it clean."

"Shit is a bad word," he says easily to his mother, and she snorts out a laugh.

"It is, baby, so don't repeat it again, okay?" She ruffles his hair.

I feel pretty confident that I'll end up getting a kiss in the end anyway, but why not make it interesting.

"I bet you can't knock down more than four pins," I tell Zoe. "Same stakes."

Zoe pouts. "You know I'm not very good at this."

I shrug. "Then you'll just have to kiss a frog."

She sighs heavily. "I guess so. Woe is me."

Elijah has this big smile on his face and I wonder why. He looks a little sly, swinging his feet back and forth as he sits in the chair.

Zoe lines up, holding her ball all wrong, but then she shifts and puts her fingers into the holes. She throws the ball smoothly, hitting a perfect strike.

I gape at her. "You... you *hustled* me."

"Only a little," she admits, and gives me a sound kiss on the mouth anyway.

Zoe bowls a *much* better game than I do and instead of being a sore loser like usual, I just feel elated. She's so great, and it just continues to get better.

I can't wait to see where this goes, but there's also a big part of me that is yelling at me to stop, to slow down.

Nothing lasts forever, a voice in the back of my head says. *Don't get too attached, because it'll just break you in the end.*

Chapter 22

Zoe

Going on dates with Jackson and Elijah has been wonderful, but I'm definitely missing our alone time, so I'm glad when the next concert comes up in a week. Elijah tells me to record part of the concert because he wants to see "Mr. Jack" sing, and I can't tell him no. I love that he and Jackson get along so well, but it also hurts, aches somewhere deep inside me that I can't tell him that Jackson's his father.

At least, not yet. Elijah is young enough that he probably won't hate me for lying to him, but I definitely can't say the same for Jackson. I feel this impending dread, like I know that everything's going to end, going to go all wrong, and I just keep putting it off.

Gemma and I ride together while Locke takes the tour bus, just so that we can have some girl time. We haven't gotten to spend nearly enough time together.

"So, without going into any amount of detail, because ew, how are things going with my brother?" Gemma asks casually after we drop Elijah off at my mother's.

I laugh. "It's going well, I guess."

"You know he's head over heels for you, right?"

I freeze. "No, he isn't. We're just dating. It's casual, or whatever."

"Or whatever?" Gemma raises an eyebrow but keeps her eyes on the road. "Jackson falls hard and fast, and he was sprung for you a long time ago, Zoe."

"Really?" My heart rate is speeding up, maybe flipping over in my chest, I don't know. I've never actually considered that Jackson might be falling in love with me. I guess it's because I've always been in love with him, so I can't imagine seeing the signs in the man I've longed for my entire life.

"Absolutely," Gemma agrees. "He's crazy about you. But you've *got* to tell him about Elijah before he gets in even deeper."

I swallow hard, unable to believe what she's saying about Jackson being in love with me, but also dreading this conversation about Elijah.

"He'll hate me if I tell him," I mourn.

"He might," Gemma says gently. "But he'll hate you more if you keep it from him for any longer."

That certainly doesn't make me feel any better, and I'm quiet for a long moment as we drive to Dallas.

"I'll tell him after the tour, just like I promised," I finally say.

Gemma glances at me. "I don't know that you can wait that long, Zoe. Jackson's getting in deeper every day, and you'll break his heart if you wait too long to tell him. If you tell him now, maybe you two can salvage things, but if you keep waiting..."

"After the tour," I say firmly. "It's the only way. I don't want to distract him, his music is more important."

"More important than you? Than his son?" Gemma asks, but I don't have an answer to that question.

Luckily, she knows me well enough to know that I need the subject dropped, so she starts to chat about Cain and Locke and how well she thinks the tour is going to go.

I listen, smiling. She's always been the talkative one while I've been a little more introverted, and it's nearly a ten-hour trip, so it's good that she and I are talking. We'll be flying out to Montgomery, Alabama, next week, and then the week after will be the show in Atlanta. After that, it's back home to Albuquerque and the final show.

I've got roughly a month to tell Jackson that I've been hiding his son from him, lying to him, all this time. I have no idea how I'm going to do it.

* * *

The concert goes great, and Jackson plays *Baby Blue* all over again, and I have to admit that I love that he changed the title to be the same as the nickname he had for me, based on my blue hair and blue eyes.

The blue hair had been a big change, but I had to change *something* after what happened with my father. I had to change a lot of things, because I needed to become a different person, not someone who was that broken.

I think I've done a pretty good job reinventing myself, becoming Zoe instead of stupid little Susie, and sometimes, I'm proud of myself. Other times, I wonder about my father and if there's anything else I could have done to help him. To protect him from himself.

I don't know why my father is so heavy on my mind lately. I guess it's because, in a way, Jackson reminds me of him. All the good things, of course, but also the tendency to numb out their feelings with booze and partying. Jackson seems so much better now, but so did my father, for a while...

I'm listening to Axel's guitar solo on the song he'd penned, *Amped Up*, and I smile and focus on Jackson, who winks at me from the stage, sweeping his sweaty hair back from his forehead.

God, he looks so *good* up there. He's really in his element when he's performing, and it's wonderful to see. I never got to see him like that when I was younger, because the band wasn't performing regularly. I'm so glad that he's living his dream. I'm so proud of him.

That pride plus the filthy martini Gemma buys me makes me grab his hand as soon as he hops down off the stage after their last encore. He's breathing hard, chugging water, but I can't wait to get him alone.

I lean up to yell/whisper in his ear over the club music which has begun again after the set. "Meet me in the bathroom."

Jackson raises an eyebrow but grins, and when I tug him inside, he mock gasps.

"Zoe, I didn't know you were this kind of girl," he teases.

"Yes, you did," I laugh, and then I push him into the stall, putting his back against the door as I lock it.

I run my hands into his shirt, popping buttons of the very outfit I'd picked out, and Jackson moans when my nails drag along his pecs. I deftly unbutton his pants, a pair of pinstripe slacks that I thought would pair well with the black boots and white button-up shirt I'd picked out for him. I lean up to nibble his earlobe, my tongue catching on the dangling zipper earring I'd given him as an accessory.

"Fuck, *Zoe*," he pants, and when I get his slacks undone and pull him out of his underwear, he moans as I wrap my fingers around him. His hands go to my hips, like he's going to pick me up, but I take a step back, shaking my head and licking my lips.

I crouch down, go down on my knees in a Dallas club bathroom, and I'm sure it's dirty but I don't care, I feel dirty tonight, naughty in a way that only Jackson has ever made me feel.

When I take him into my mouth he jerks his head back so hard that his head bangs against the stall door and I giggle around him, taking him deeper and deeper until I gag.

At the sound of my gag his hips jut forward and I do it again, almost on purpose this time, because I love the way he reacts.

"Oh, God, your *mouth*," he moans, and I flatten my tongue, covering my teeth as he fucks into my throat. Even with his most precious body part in my mouth, he's in control, thrusting his hips forward, his hand in my hair, not pushing but just slowly sliding into my mouth.

"You're so fucking pretty with my cock in your mouth," he murmurs. "Look at how those pretty blue eyes are watering. You take me so well, baby blue."

His words send a shock right through me, pooling heat between my thighs, and I move my head faster and faster until he gasps, fists his hand in my hair and spills into my mouth, hot and slightly salty. He tastes good and I look up at him, opening my mouth to show that I'm keeping his come on my tongue, and his dick twitches in my hand.

"Dirty girl," he murmurs, his green eyes dark with lust, and I swallow. He still has his hand in my hair, and he jerks me up and it stings in just the right way. He kisses me hard and dirty, tasting himself on my tongue, and I've never wanted him inside me so badly as I do right that moment.

"Zoe, you're going to miss your flight," Gemma yells.

"I'm not coming in because I don't want to have to bleach my eyeballs, but I've got to take you to the airport."

Jackson frowns. "I thought your flight was in the morning."

I shake my head. "Had to get a red-eye because it was the only one available. I need to get back to Elijah."

"We're going to be driving the rest of the way," Jackson pouts. "I won't be able to see you."

I smile. "I'll call you and we can facetime."

Jackson grins. "Dirty facetime?"

"Absolutely," I agree, and I kiss him again, adjusting him back into his pants. I smooth down my hair and as I go to unlock the door, Jackson grabs my wrist.

"Zoe," he says. "Baby blue."

His green eyes are so serious now and I swallow hard, wondering what he's going to say.

"I'm falling in love with you."

Chapter 23

Jackson

*Z*oe stares up at me with huge blue eyes. They seem to take up her whole face. She looks shocked, and I can't imagine why. I figured it's pretty obvious how I feel about her, how crazy I am about her, but maybe I haven't been as obvious as I thought.

"Jackson," she breathes, and I wait for her to say it back, to say she's falling for me too, but instead, she leaves the bathroom stall and strides out of the bathroom, meeting my sister in the hall.

"Zoe!" I call, but she's gone and she can't hear me over the music anyway and my dick is still halfway out of my slacks. I curse, adjusting my clothes, and then slam my fist on the bathroom stall.

A woman stumbles in, her mascara streaked and she gapes at me.

"Oh shit, you're Jack from Jack and the Spades," she says, and it's still weird that people recognize me sometimes. I'm only semi-famous in a few states, but it's an odd experience nonetheless.

I wink at her. "I am. Have a good night, ma'am." I fake a

southern accent since we're in Texas, after all, and she just stares at me as I run out into the club, looking for Zoe.

Instead, I find Axel, half drunk and talking to Harley on the phone.

"What's she doing now?" I heard him ask.

Axel seems to think that every concert Jazz doesn't come with us, he'll miss some kind of milestone, but she's still little enough that he probably won't miss much. This is just a mini-tour, anyway, so he should be home before any of the big milestones.

Locke is at the bar, drinking a club soda because he doesn't drink much without Gemma around, and I glumly sit next to him on a barstool and order my own club soda with lemon and lime. It's the closest thing to the vodka and soda that I'm craving.

"Zoe and Gemma got out of here quick," he comments.

"Yeah," I mumble. "Zoe was probably trying to get away from me."

Locke frowns, looking around at all the liquor and I know what he's thinking. He's thinking that if I'm in this kind of mood, I might go back to drinking, and I can't blame him.

"Why don't we go get something to eat? Samuel's driving Axel back to his hotel, but ours is close enough to walk. I could use the cool air, it's hot as hell in here," Locke suggests, and I nod.

On the walk to a nearby all-night diner, Locke doesn't talk much, and I appreciate my friend's close-mouthed way of dealing with things. He's more a man of action than words, and he probably wouldn't give me the same kind of attitude that his wife did.

My baby sister would tell me to back off, but I'm hoping that my friends, my brothers, will have a different reaction.

"What'd you do?" Locke asks after we order and I roll my eyes.

Well, there goes my hope that my best friend would understand me.

"I didn't do anything!" I insist. "I just told her that I'm falling in love with her. What's so bad about that?"

Locke chokes on his water. "You told her that *already?*"

"Just because it took you like, two months and a surprise baby to realize you were in love with my sister doesn't mean we're all like you, Locke," I say, and Locke groans.

"I know that you fall easily, but how long have you even known this girl? You only spent a bit of time together on the last tour, right?" Locke asks.

"Yeah, but I've known her my whole life!" I protest, and Locke gives me a look.

"You didn't even remember her until recently."

"I didn't *recognize* her. I remembered her," I correct him, and Locke shrugs.

"I don't know, man, maybe she's one of those types that takes a while to open up. She seems a little introverted. And didn't you kind of break her heart when she was a kid? Jackson, come on. There are a lot of reasons she could be scared."

"I know," I say, sighing. "It's too soon, and she's got a kid, and I get that can be tough with dating."

The food comes quickly, and Locke attacks his fries and I attack my burger. We're always starving after concerts. Luckily, the denizens of this little Dallas diner have no earthly idea who Jack and the Spades are, so we don't get recognized or anything. I like being famous, or at least a little famous, but sometimes, I just want to be left alone. Especially when I'm in a mood like this.

"And you said the father's not in the picture?" Locke asks, and I raise an eyebrow.

"Why would you ask that?"

Locke shrugs, a habit he has that kind of drives me nuts. "I don't know. If Gemma had a baby daddy I'd be freaking out about her talking to him."

I frown. "Yeah, she says she's still in contact with him. I even overheard her telling Samuel that her baby's father wanted to get back together."

Locke's mouth drops open, a fry falling out. "Shit, really? So, is she seeing him?"

I rub a hand against the back of my neck. "She says she isn't. God, I hope not," I mumble. That would be heart-breaking in a completely different way than her just being slow to open up.

"When would she even have time? With all the tour stuff and dating you, she's busy, right? And she's a single mom," Locke offers.

I nod, smiling, but then I pale when I really think about it.

"I won't see her for the weekend every week this month," I say, and Locke stares at me.

"So?"

"So? All that time she could be talking to her ex!" I bang my fist on the table, a little dramatic, even I can admit.

"You're talking yourself into a spiral, Jackson, stop it," Locke warns. "She says she's not seeing him, so believe her. You trust her, right?"

Do I trust her? I guess I do. It's not like I've ever been cheated on or anything, not exactly, anyway. Maria broke up with me because I was becoming a rockstar and I was a mess (so she said) but then she immediately married a drummer who had at least as bad a reputation as me. It isn't that I think Zoe would cheat, especially since we've already said we're exclusive, but talking isn't cheating, is it?

And I bet that bastard will be talking to her, trying to butter her up, trying to weasel his way back into her life. I tell myself that I wouldn't have a problem with him wanting to be in Elijah's life, but I know that will drive me nuts, too, especially if he's still after Zoe. And who wouldn't be? She's wonderful.

"I trust her," I say finally, and Locke hums in the back of his throat.

"Then you've got nothing to worry about. Just back off with the I love you shit, okay? Just for a while. Give her until the end of the tour, at least."

I take in a deep breath through my nostrils. "Okay. You're right. I need to just back off a little."

"A lot," Locke complains. "Just keep things casual for now."

"All right, all right, fair enough," I mumble, but I'm not quite sure how I'm going to do that. I'm already itching to call her and she's only been gone a couple of hours.

I may or may not take Locke's advice, because I'm just a mess that way, but I'm glad he gave it to me nonetheless.

"Thanks for the advice," I tell him earnestly, and he smiles.

"You're welcome. I could have used some about Gemma when I was in your situation, so I figured It would be good karma."

"What, to balance out that you knocked up my little sister behind my back?" I drawl.

"Exactly," Locke points at me, and we both burst out laughing.

I'm terrified that I'm in love again. It's the first time since Maria, since she put my heart in a blender and poured it down the sink, and I don't want to spiral like that ever again. Zoe wouldn't hurt me, though, would she? I could trust her?

I don't know what to do about Zoe, but laughing with Locke feels good.

No matter what is going on in my love life, I always have my brothers.

Chapter 24

Zoe

"What's going on with you?" Gemma asks the second we're in the car on the way to the airport.

I bite at my cuticle, trying to decide if I should tell her or not. I feel as if she'll be mad at me because she's been telling me that Jackson has been falling for me, but it's just so hard to believe. It's like it's too good to be true, or something.

"You only bite your cuticle when you're nervous," Gemma warns, "so I know something's up."

"He told me he was in love with me," I say softly, and Gemma groans and bangs her hands against the steering wheel.

"Damnit, Zoe, I *told* you," she complains.

"I know, I *know!*" I wail.

"What are you gonna do now, Zoe? You have to *tell* him."

"I can't," I whisper. "He's going to hate me. Everything's going to go wrong."

"You've been lying to him all this time, Zoe, and the

longer it goes on, the less likely he's going to be to forgive you," Gemma warns, and I know that she's right.

My lip trembles. "I still love him, Gem. Just as much as I ever did. I don't want to lose him."

Gemma pulls into the airport and puts a hand on my shoulder while cars are honking at us to hurry. She puts up her middle finger, smiling at the people yelling, and gives me a big hug.

"Just think about it for the next concert. Tell him after, in person. He deserves to know, and you both deserve the chance to be happy."

I sniffle and hug her back tightly before getting out to grab my luggage bag and hurry to bag check.

The flight home is only about ninety minutes, and I look out the window, thinking the whole time about what I'm going to do. Jackson doesn't know that Elijah is his son, but he also doesn't know so many other things. We'd spent so much time apart. We don't know much about each other anymore, and I want that to change.

I figure it would change, if we kept dating. I wish I just had a little more time. I wish I could explain to him why I felt the way that I did. I want him to know that I love him *so much* but that I'm afraid of being broken again. I don't think I can start over again. Zoe is who I am now, and I want Jackson to know me and my history. If we'd just dated back *then*, everything would be different.

But everything isn't different. Back home, it's nearing four in the morning when I finally lie down in my bed, planning to pick Elijah up in the morning. I stare up at the ceiling, thinking, and then startle when my phone starts to buzz.

It's Jackson, facetiming me, and I frown, sliding open the phone.

The light of the lamp of the hotel makes Jackson visible, shirtless, his abs on display and my mouth goes dry. His long, light brown hair is slicked back from the shower and he looks so good I could lick the screen.

"You're calling so late. You haven't been drinking, have you?" I ask, not meaning to be accusatory but not able to help it.

Jackson shakes his head. "Not drinking," he murmurs. "Just thinking about you."

Heat spreads through my body. "I just left, though."

"Doesn't matter," he says in a low voice, sliding his hand down his abdomen to the waistband of his boxer briefs. "I always think about you."

"What do you think about?" I ask, my breath coming closer.

He pouts. "No more answering questions until you turn a light on. I want to see you."

I flip on the lamp beside my bed and squint at the change. Jackson breaks out in a half-smile.

"There's my girl." He pauses. "You *are* my girl, right?"

I lick my lips, staring at him. "I'm your girl, Jackson. I'm all yours," I say again, knowing that he loves to hear it, and he groans and I realize that just below the camera, he's groping himself through his underwear.

"Jackson, what are you doing?" I ask, pretending to be scandalized.

"Wishing it was your fingers wrapped around me," he rasps, and I gasp, sitting back against the pillows and teasing one of my nipples through my old, ratty T-shirt.

"I wish my fingers were yours, too," I admit, and Jackson hisses in a breath, tilting his camera down so I can see him stroking himself.

"I want to see you," he says, biting his lip. "Show me your tits."

I pull up my shirt, holding it with my teeth and baring my breasts, and Jackson gets closer to the camera before dropping it on the floor.

I hear him curse and I giggle as he picks it up.

"Got too excited," he jokes. "But I want to see more. I want to see how you play with yourself, baby blue. Can you put the phone on the nightstand and show me?"

Fuck. That sounds like the hottest thing I've ever heard, and it will definitely be the hottest thing I've ever done.

"I'll try," I manage, and I prop it up using the lamp and then turn to face the camera, spreading my legs and feeling oddly shy.

I moan and reach down to slip my thumb over my clit, and Jackson tsks in the back of his throat.

"Did I say you could do that, baby blue? I'm calling the shots here, so ask my permission."

Oh, fuck. I love it when he takes control like this, and I'm so slick that I'm sure I'm soaking through my panties.

"Can I please touch myself?" I plead. "Just a little?"

"Not yet," he demands, and I sigh and move my hands back up to my breasts. I begin to tease my nipples, almost hoping he will scold me about that too. Instead, he's looking right between my legs.

"Oh fuck, look at you," he gasps. "Spread yourself open for me," he demands, and I'm blushing but I can't look away, looking into his lust-filled green eyes and spreading myself with my fingers in a "V."

Jackson moans loudly, staring right at my pussy, his full mouth slightly open. "God, I wish I could taste you," he continues. "I wish I could stick my fingers inside you, make you come."

161

"I could pretend my fingers are yours," I moan. "Please, Jackson, let me touch myself."

"Slide your fingers over your clit," he commands, and I do as he says, gasping, using one hand to continue to twist one of my nipples between my fingers. I'm so close to coming it's ridiculous, just from his voice over the phone, the way he's looking at me and bossing me around.

"Can you fit two fingers in, baby blue?" he asks softly, and I do so, arching my back and crying out. "I bet you can fit more. I know you can. You always take my cock so well," he murmurs, and after a moment I'm able to fit three fingers, pumping them in and out, unable to stop myself. Jackson doesn't scold me, though, his hoarse breathing all I can hear over the phone.

"Come with me," I beg him, looking into his eyes and he tilts the phone down again so that I can see him pumping his fists, pre-ejaculate coating his fingers. He's just as close as I am.

"I'm coming, baby, fuck, fuck," he curses, and as I watch him spill all over his hand and belly, I come around my own fingers, wishing it was him inside me instead, wishing I could feel his dick pulse inside me.

"Oh my God," I groan when I finally clean up and get back on the phone, looking at him with flushed cheeks. "I've never done that before."

Jackson grins. "I can't say the same, but I can say I don't think I've ever come that hard by myself. That was all you, baby blue."

I grin back at him. I love hearing that, love hearing how much I pleasure him. It's a huge ego boost. Jackson's good at giving those.

He looks at me fondly, a soft smile on his face, and I frown a little.

"Jack, I'm sorry that I didn't say anything when you told me—"

Jackson shakes his head. "No, it's okay," he promises. "It was too soon. I overwhelmed you."

"A little," I admit. "But it's not too soon, Jackson. You know that I feel the same way."

"Do I know that?" he asks softly, searching my face through the phone screen.

"You should. I've been crazy about you since I was sixteen."

"After what I did to you, I don't know why," he says glumly, and I smile at him.

"You were a different guy then. I was a different girl. You're a new Jackson, and I'm Zoe instead of Susie, right?"

Jackson grins. "Right. So, does that mean I can tell you that I love you?" he asks, and it takes my breath and I flush again.

"I don't know, that might give me heart palpitations," I laugh. "Let's take it a little slow for now, okay?"

Jackson nods, looking exhausted all of a sudden. He yawns so big that it cracks his jaw.

"Will you tell me just one time?" he asks, looking at me again so fondly that it makes my heart ache.

"Tell you what?"

"You know."

I smile and take in a deep breath, saying something that I've always felt but never imagined that I could say to him.

"I love you too, Jackson."

* * *

The next week goes by in a blur without Jackson, because Elijah is starting pre-school and there's a million things to do. Jackson texts me every day, and almost every night we talk on the phone, although he's been too tired for facetime play again. That's too bad, because it had been phenomenal.

I miss him viscerally, and I'm feeling such an amount of dread about telling him about Elijah that it makes me feel sick and I am barely able to eat all week. I know that Jackson loves me now, but how will he feel when I tell him that I've been lying to him all this time? He's going to hate me, and it'll ruin everything, and I wish that I could just disappear.

The flight to Montgomery is a bit longer, and I tear up my cuticles just thinking about what will happen after the concert. Tonight is the night that Gemma made me promise to tell him, and I know she'll tell him if I don't.

I haven't explained anything to Elijah, because for all I know, Jackson might disappear as soon as he finds out he's the father. I don't like to think about it, but I have no idea what he'll do when he finds out.

I drop off all the guy's clothes slowly, and Gemma gives me a look that tells me that I better tell Jackson tonight or else. I hang around at Samuel's hotel room, biting at my cuticle, and he looks over at me.

"That's going to get infected," he says, and I nod. I know, and they often do, but it's just a habit I haven't been able to break.

"Do you remember what I told you about the father of my child?" I ask, and Samuel rolls his eyes a little.

"Am I still supposed to be pretending I don't know it's Jackson?" he asks dryly, and I have to admit, I'm not surprised.

Samuel's pretty astute, like Gemma, and I assumed he'd done the math.

"No," I say with a soft chuckle, "but I think he's going to leave me when I tell him."

Samuel frowns. "Jackson wouldn't leave his family. You've known him for years, you should know that."

I bite at my cuticle some more. Do I know Jackson well enough for that? He's always been so loyal to Gemma, such a good brother to her. Surely he'll be a good father, too, but that doesn't mean he won't leave *me*. It doesn't mean he'll always be a good father. That's what I wish I could explain to Jackson.

I finally make it to Jackson's hotel room, and he frowns at me as soon as I knock on the door.

"Gemma said you booked your own room? Why? Are you mad at me about something?" he asks, looking concerned.

I shake my head. "No. Just have something I need to talk to you about, tonight," I answer him, but that doesn't seem to make him feel any better.

Jackson takes my hand as I go to turn away, cradling his outfit for the night in his other hand.

"Baby blue," he pleads. "Tell me what's wrong."

"After the concert," I say gently, and pull away from him. Jackson's searching my face, still frowning, but I can't tell him now. If I tell him now, he'll never make it to the concert, and fans in Montgomery can be a little rowdy, according to Gemma.

Tonight is the night my whole life is going to change.

Chapter 25

Jackson

In some of the worst times of my life, I've performed and not missed cues. I've performed drunk, hungover, and everything in between and managed to hit every cue, but tonight, I'm off. My voice is flat in some places, and I miss two cues before the first set is even over. I want to find Zoe during the break, but she's nowhere to be seen. Gemma's acting weird, and all I can do is sit over at the bar and drink my soda water with lemon and lime. Samuel's looking at me like I'm going to hop over the bar and drink the bottles in the speed rail, and since he's the one of the Spades closest to Zoe, I'm worried that this is bad news.

If it isn't bad news, why would she wait until after the concert? My chest feels tight, my throat aching. I hate this. I hate this anxiety more than I will hate whatever she has to tell me. Or maybe I'm wrong. Maybe she's going to tell me that it's over, that she's getting back together with Elijah's father, and I'll wish for this anxiety.

When I finally see Zoe, she's in the hallway with Gemma, crying, and I swear I don't mean to eavesdrop but whispering in a club is like whispering in a sawmill–you can't really do it, so they're yelling over the music.

"You *have* to tell him, Zo. I'm sorry."

"I don't know if I can," Zoe sobs, and I dart around the corner so that she can't see me.

What *is* it? She has to be breaking up with me. This has to be about the father, especially with the way that Samuel is acting. I feel like my heart is sinking to my toes every minute that goes by, but I don't know what to do about it. I just keep telling myself I'll be okay, even if it's the worst thing, even if it's true that nothing lasts forever.

The second the concert is over I find Zoe immediately, tugging her outside without even helping the guys put the equipment up or take it to the truck.

"What's going on?" I ask firmly, and my voice doesn't break.

"I can't tell you here," Zoe hisses, pulling away from me and wiping at her eyes.

"Where, then?" I ask, shifting my weight from one foot to the other. I feel like I'm full to bursting and with what, I can't say. Anxiety. Dread. Panic.

"Back at the hotel," she says. "I was going to ride with everyone."

I lock my jaw. "Why wait?" I ask her, just *knowing* she's going to break up with me. "I know what you're going to say."

Zoe's blue eyes shoot to mine. "What do you mean, you know? Did Gemma tell you?"

"No, but I can guess. You're choosing him, right? Elijah's father?"

Zoe stares at me for a long moment. "Jackson, it's so much more complicated than that."

"I don't think it's very complicated at all," I say, my

voice rising. "You lead me on, let me think that we could be something, and all the time you've been talking to your ex, planning on getting your family back together. That's it, isn't it?"

"Jackson, I can't do this right now," she says, and heads back inside.

I yell and bang my fist on the hood of the tour bus, feeling about twenty emotions at once. If Gemma notices the dent I left, she doesn't say anything, just pats me on the shoulder and climbs onto the tour bus.

The ride, which is only about fifteen minutes, seems to take forever, and Zoe won't even look at me. I want to take her hand but I'm still so *mad* and I don't even know if I'm mad for the right reasons. I can't think of anything else she might possibly have to tell me, and given that Gemma and Samuel are treating me with kid gloves...

I try to think of any other explanation, but I can't. All I can think is that she's going to leave me, and my heart is pre-emptively breaking. I hate this. I *hate* this. I hate feeling like I'm worthless, like I'm nothing, like I'm not good enough. The reason I'd barely had any relationship since Maria is because heartbreak hits me hard. I'm not gonna pretend to be a tough guy and say it doesn't bother me—breakups rip me in half, and they have since I was a kid. I still remember the first time I got rejected, when my middle school crush chose the football player over me.

Gemma and Locke get off on the second floor, and Samuel and Axel on the third, so it's just me and Zoe going up to my fifth-floor hotel room and she's not speaking to me. She's not even looking at me.

"Zoe," I say just as the elevator doors open, and she doesn't respond, just following me silently to my room as I unlock the door. She's still crying. I feel like my chest might implode, like I've got broken ribs or something, it hurts so much.

She sits down on the bed, and I can't stand to sit, running my fingers through my hair and pacing around the room.

"Jackson," she starts, and I go toward her, my heart rate speeding up, because suddenly I don't want her to say it.

"Don't say it," I mourn, kissing along her face, crouching in front of her. "Don't say it, baby blue, okay? If you don't say it, then..."

"I have to say it," she whispers, and I kiss the tears from her face before kissing her mouth, soft and sweet. She sobs into my mouth and pushes me away.

"Zoe, I love you," I say brokenly, tears springing to the backs of my eyes. "Don't leave me."

"I don't want to leave you," she manages in a shaking voice. "But you might want to leave me."

I rock back on my haunches, staring at her. "What happened?" I ask, my heart beating ever harder.

Has she cheated? Did she fuck him when we were apart for this week? I think if that's what she says next I'm going to throw something through the hotel wall, find out the guy's name and rip his head off, possibly.

"I've been lying to you," she whispers, and God, my stomach hurts, I think I'm going to be sick.

"I've never wanted to drink so much as I do this very second," I say thickly, and it's true. I want to open up the minibar and destroy everything in there, numb out the way I'm feeling right now.

"Don't say that, Jackson," she sobs. "You can't go back to drinking because of me. Because of this."

"Because of *what*, Zoe? You have to tell me, I'm going crazy," I plead, and I take both of her hands in mine.

Zoe looks at me with those big blue eyes, tears streaming down her face.

"You're Elijah's father."

I'd thought that her telling me she cheated on me, that she was leaving me, would break me. But nothing could break me more than what she's saying now.

"No, I'm not," I say dumbly, and Zoe nods her head.

"You are. I got pregnant that first time, when I was seventeen, and—"

"And you didn't tell me," I say incredulously, anger rising inside me. "You didn't tell me and you've been lying to me all this time."

"Jackson, I'm sorry. I'm *so* sorry, you don't understand—"

I rip my hands away from her and stand up, running my hand through my hair again to get it out of my face.

"You're damn right I don't understand," I burst out. "What was it? Why wouldn't you *tell* me that I have a son?"

"Because you wouldn't have been a good father!" Zoe nearly yells, and then claps her hand over her mouth.

My heart hurts so much I'm actually worried it might be a heart condition, and then finally, blissfully, my walls come up and I go numb and cold all over. It feels like it did when they told me my parents were dead at the hospital, like I'm watching myself from outside my body somehow.

"I would have gotten it together," I insist. "I got it together *anyway*. I'm better now. I'm different. And I would have been different for you, for Elijah."

"Jackson, I'm sorry, I shouldn't have said that, but you have to understand—" Zoe stands up, moving toward me with her arms extended but I back away.

"I understand," I say coldly. "I understand that you didn't think I was good enough then, and you don't think

I'm good enough now. You think I'd just have abandoned you, fucked off to go drink and party if I knew I had a kid?"

"I don't know," she wails. "Jackson, my father—"

I only vaguely know the situation with Zoe's father, but right now I don't care. Right now I can't listen to a single other thing that comes out of her mouth.

"I'm not your father," I bark. "I'm Elijah's father, and he deserved to know me. I deserved to know *him*, Zoe!"

"You're right," she sniffles. "You're right and we can fix this, right?" Her voice trembles and sounds almost desperate, and I want to give in, want to take her into my arms and tell her it'll all be okay but I'm so *angry*.

"There's no fixing this," I say softly, calmly. "Get out."

"Jackson, don't shut me out," Zoe says, and I point to the door.

"Get. Out."

She leaves, and sound of the door closing behind her makes me want to punch walls, to trash the hotel room like a real rockstar. I stare at the minibar for a long, long time.

But I'm a father now. I'm a father now, and Zoe's a liar, and everything's turned upside down but I want to be a good man for my son.

171

Chapter 26

Zoe

Of all the ways I imagined being with Jackson Arden when I was a teenager, I never thought I'd be the one to break his heart.

Jackson's devastated, and I don't know how I thought it would be otherwise. Part of me had hoped that he would be happy, that he'd say *"Sure, no problem, Zoe. I love you and Elijah, and I understand why you lied."*

That's delusional at best, and some part of me knows that, but nothing has ever hurt so much in my life than seeing the tears in Jackson's eyes, the hurt flashing across his handsome face before he shut down.

Not even when he'd talked about Maria the day after we first made love.

He's never going to talk to me again, and although my best friend is in the same hotel as I am, I can't go to her crying over what I've done to her brother. I'm surprised that she hasn't already cut me out as a stylist for the Spades and her best friend.

When there's a knock on my hotel room, I run for it, hoping against hope that it'll be Jackson.

Instead, it's Gemma, with mint chocolate ice cream and a bottle of wine.

"Gem," I gasp, pulling her inside and into a hug. She puts everything down before hugging me back tightly. "I didn't want to come to your room, I thought you'd be mad at me."

"I *am* mad at you," she says firmly. "But you're still my best friend, and I love you even when you fuck up."

My broken heart swells when I think about how she's there for me even though I've done terrible things, and I start to sob. She hugs me again before opening up the ice cream and offering me a spoon.

"The only way through it is through it, Zoe. I can't tell you that Jackson is going to come around. He might, but family is really important to him."

I nod, still crying.

"He's hurt that you didn't tell him, that he missed out on so much of Elijah's life. Just give him some time," she offers gently, but I know she's wrong. She's just trying to make me feel better. Jackson will probably never speak to me again.

* * *

I'm wrong about Jackson never speaking to me again. He facetimes me before the concert the next day, and I'm so shocked I run to the bathroom to splash water on my puffy face before I answer.

Jackson looks at me but it's like there's nothing behind his eyes, just cold. Empty.

"I was hoping I could talk to Elijah," he says, and I nod numbly.

"I, uh, haven't told him yet," I start.

Jackson scoffs. "Of course you haven't." He pauses and takes in a deep breath. "We'll wait until after the tour, tell him together."

"We will?" I ask hopefully.

"Of course. We're his family, Zoe, even if we aren't together."

Oh. That's what he means. That we'll be civil with each other for Elijah's sake. Of course, he doesn't mean he wants to be with *me*. Why would he want that? I'm a liar, a manipulator. I've taken away Elijah's childhood from him. Those are all things Gemma made me realize the other night. I've been in the wrong, and I don't know how to make it all okay again.

"Jackson, can we talk?" I ask, and he just stares at me.

"No. I just want to see my son," he says flatly, and so I give the phone to Elijah, who's in his room playing with Legos.

He shows "Mr. Jack" all his buildings and the castle fort he made for his stuffed animals, and they talk about the concert and everything that happened. Jackson is laughing, his voice cheery, so different than he was with me.

When I get back on the phone, he's already hung up.

What the hell am I going to do?

The weeks that Jack and the Spades and Gemma are on tour feel so long now that I'm not talking to Jackson. I call Gemma almost every night, and I think she's getting tired of hearing the same old thing.

"He won't talk to me," I wail one night after drinking two glasses of wine after Elijah went to bed.

"He will when we get back. He'll have to," she assures me. "He keeps telling me all about Elijah and their conversations. Don't you get to talk to him, then?"

"No," I mumble. "He just hangs up as soon as he and Elijah are done talking."

"Are you still texting him?"

I bite my cuticle. "Just once a day," I say, and that much is true. I keep asking if we can talk, and he keeps responding with a simple: *no*.

"Zoe, it's going to be okay. Either way," Gemma says gently, but it doesn't feel like it's going to be okay.

"How's he doing?" I ask.

"If you're asking if he's drinking, he's not," Gemma says, but without any judgment. Gemma, more than anyone, understands why I worry about Jackson.

I sigh in relief. "Good." I would never want to be the reason he started drinking and partying again, numbing himself out just because I'd hurt him. Jackson's better than that, though, now. He's a good man, and I've just been an idiot.

Without Jackson, I don't know how to function anymore, it seems. Gemma let me out of styling the guys at the Atlanta show before they come home for the final home-town show, and she paid me in full anyway, so I don't have any work to do. I have nothing to do but play with Elijah during the day and cry at night.

Even my kid has been noticing that I'm not doing very well.

"You look puffy, mommy," he tells me, and I do my best to smile at him. I don't know how the first meeting is going to go, how Elijah is going to take it, and I'm dreading seeing Jackson again just as much as I'm excited to see him.

I expect Jackson to show up a couple days after they get back from Atlanta, maybe a week, but instead, he shows up at my front stoop the day they return, around ten in the morning.

His eyes are bloodshot and I can tell he hasn't slept. He's dressed nicely in slacks and a button-up, though, his hair freshly washed like he wants to look good for Elijah, and it makes me smile although I hide it with my hand.

"Jackson," I say, and a muscle in his jaw twitches.

"Zoe," he responds simply, and walks in past me. "Where's Elijah?"

I warned Elijah that this would be a big day, and he's excited.

"What are we doing today? Are we playing with Mr. Jack?" he asks as I carry him into the living room where Jackson is sitting.

"We are, but we have something to tell you," I say, and God, I hope my son doesn't hate me for this when he's older. I sit Elijah down next to Jackson and I sit on the other side of him.

"You know how you ask me why you don't have a daddy sometimes?" I ask, and I see something flash in Jackson's green eyes, anger or hurt or both.

Elijah nods.

"You do have a daddy. Mr. Jack is your daddy," I finally manage, and Elijah's green eyes widen and he turns to look at Jackson.

"You're my daddy?" he asks, and Jackson's crying, silent tears streaming down his face.

"Yeah, buddy," he says, his voice cracking. "I'm your daddy."

Elijah, sweet little soul that he is, takes no time accepting it and throws himself into his father's arms. Jackson squeezes him tight, looking at me over Elijah's shoulder. I'm crying too, now, and I've never imagined this moment. I thought I'd keep this secret forever, but it's so sweet I can barely stand it. I should have done this so many years ago.

"Does that mean you're going to live here with me and mommy?" Elijah chirps, and Jackson clears his throat.

"I don't know, buddy. We have to work everything out, and it might take some time, but I want to see you almost every day. Is that okay with you?"

"Sure, Mr. Jack." Elijah looks at him shyly. "I mean, sure, daddy."

Jackson's face tightens and he chokes back a sob before hugging Elijah again.

Elijah doesn't seem concerned about how everyone's crying, climbing down to play, and Jackson and I share a look that isn't cold, for once, that's just happy to be looking at our son, but then the walls come back up and Jackson shuts down all over again.

I met my Prince Charming when I was sixteen years old, but look how it all ended up.

Chapter 27

Jackson

I love being a father. I absolutely love seeing my son build elaborate houses out of Legos and jam out to music on his little fake guitar. I'm over at Zoe's enough to give him a bath at night, snuggle up with him in his bed when he doesn't want to sleep alone. I've spent the night a couple of times, and when I have to be away for the Albuquerque show, it hurts to say goodbye to him.

"You were gone so long, daddy," Elijah says, crying just a little. My tough little guy. "Please don't take so long this time."

I look up at Zoe, and I hate her in that moment as much as I love her. It's a conundrum, how much I love being a father and how utterly miserable I am without Zoe.

I'm snapping at everyone, barking at every little inconvenience, and when I start trying to backseat drive, Gemma pulls the car over, nearly killing all of us.

"Holy shit!" Axel yells, sliding sideways. Good thing they haven't brought the kids this time.

"What the fuck, Gemma?" I start, and she points at me.

"Don't you dare, Jackson Ezekiel Arden," she snaps. and

I wince. Not my middle name. She only uses that when she's *really* mad.

"I'm sorry," I apologize quickly, knowing that I'm the one in the wrong. "I'm being an asshole."

"You *are* being an asshole, and It's because of my best friend, and you need to *talk* to her."

"I'm not interested in anything she has to say," I say tightly.

"You don't know Zoe the way you think you do," Gemma says, glaring at me. "Because you didn't know Susie."

"They're one in the same, aren't they?" I ask, huffing out a breath, and Gemma rolls her eyes.

"Stop being stupid and talk to her when we get home. You guys at least need to figure out some kind of custody agreement. I don't see my nephew enough."

"Yeah, I haven't even met him!" Samuel argues.

I glare at Samuel. He told me that he'd done the math and had put it together that I was Elijah's father, and I'm still a little peeved that he didn't tell me right away and let Zoe do it.

I should be mad at Gemma, too, but I know they're best friends, and I know if Locke told me something important, I'd keep it from her if I had to. My loyalty in the end would be to her, but I'd keep a secret for a while to be loyal to my friend, too.

When we arrive at the hotel, I figure that it'll be Gemma who pulls me aside to give me the "don't drink" lecture, but instead, it's Axel, throwing an arm around my shoulders and leading me to his room.

"I know you're thinking about it," he accuses, and I take a deep breath.

"Of *course* I'm thinking about it. Wouldn't you be?"

"I was three sheets to the wind the whole first tour about Harley, man, yeah, I would be. I know you're upset. I know you're heartbroken. But you're a father now."

"I'm not drinking," I say, and Axel nods.

"But you're not sleeping either, are you? Staying out too late, flirting with a million girls who you wish had eyes just the same color as hers?"

I gape at him. "You really know what you're talking about."

"I went through that shit for *months* with Harley. She put me through the wringer but I can't understand why you're putting *yourself* through the wringer."

I look at him. "What the hell are you talking about?"

"You're heartbroken, right? Miserable?"

I pause and then nod, feeling no reason to lie.

"Are you miserable because Zoe lied to you or because you don't have your family together?" Axel asks, and I open my mouth to answer and then close it again.

"Shit. I don't know. Both."

Axel nods. "Yeah, both, exactly. After I found out Harley was going to be okay, I was mad too. I told her she shouldn't have lied to me, that I missed out on so much of her pregnancy. I know it's worse for you, I know you missed out on his first words and his first steps... but you still love Zoe, don't you?"

"I love her so much," I say softly. "And I hate it. I hate that I love her so much."

Axel chuckles, sitting down on the bed. "Man, I understand that. When Harley dumped me, I hated her just as much as I loved her. But you don't hate people that you don't love, Jackson. You're just indifferent. And I'll tell you from experience, forgiving her has taken time. It's taken lots of conversations and lots of work, but it's been worth it. She's always been worth it to me. Is Zoe worth it to you?"

Yes, I think, automatically. She is worth it. She's at least worth talking to, trying to get an explanation.

* * *

On the tour bus ride back from Albuquerque, after a concert that I've been somehow subconsciously looking for Zoe all night, as if she might have shown up when I wasn't paying attention, I call the mother of my child.

"I want to see you," I say and my voice is husky with lack of sleep and all the singing I've done over the past few weeks.

"Elijah has pre-school tomorrow until one," she starts, and I interrupt her.

"I want to see you without our son around. We need to talk."

Zoe's quiet for a long moment, and I know that I still sound mad because I *am* still mad, and I wonder if she'll say no.

"I'm home all day today," she says finally, and I get back into town around nine in the morning. I don't shower or sleep, just head to her place after Gemma drops me off at home, and she answers the door in a robe, also looking like she hasn't slept.

She doesn't speak, just moves aside to let me into the room, and I sit down in the recliner so that she can't sit next to me. I can't think when I can see her and smell her and feel her so close to me, not even with how angry I am.

"What do you want to talk about?" she asks meekly, and I can't look at her. I can't look at her or I'll give in right away or be even more angry, and I need to be clear-headed right now.

"Us," I say softly. "I want to talk about us, Zoe."

"I didn't think there was an us," she says, tilting her chin up slightly as if she's offended. She has no right to be, but I still find it a little bit cute.

"You said I didn't understand," I tell her. "You said that it was more complicated than I thought, and I need you to explain things to me, Zoe. I need to know why you didn't tell me, why you left town. Because if it's just that you thought I was a fuck-up, I can get that, Zoe. I can understand that. But you didn't tell me *after* you knew I was better. You lied to me for months, and that's what I need you to tell me."

Zoe sits down across from me, taking in a deep breath. "You know that my father was an alcoholic, right?"

"I do," I say tightly. I've told her before that I'm not her father.

"Did you know that he got clean?" she asks, and I blinked, surprised.

"No. No, I didn't know that."

"For two years, Jackson. He was clean for two years. I moved in with him, left mom so that I could help him out by working while he got back on his feet. He got a good job. He wasn't drinking, wasn't going out at night. He was doing so *well*, Jackson."

I swallow. "What happened?"

Zoe's lip trembles but she isn't crying, not yet.

"He relapsed. Worse. More drinking, more partying, more drugs. He left me. I didn't know where he was for days, and when I found him, he was in the hospital from an overdose. He didn't get better, Jackson. I don't even know where he is."

"Oh, God, Zoe. I'm so sorry," I say hoarsely, leaning forward but still hesitating to take her hands.

"It isn't that I don't think you're a good man, Jackson. You're the best man I know. But my father was too, when he was clean. When he chose me over the booze and drugs. I never want Elijah to have to go through that. I never want him to have to reinvent himself because he's so depressed that his father abandoned him."

"Zoe," I manage, my voice breaking. I get on my knees between her legs, looking into her eyes. "I would never, *ever* abandon you or Elijah. I know that I've been a fuckup in the past, but I was never an addict. I know it's a slippery slope. I know that I tend to go off the rails when I'm feeling a certain kind of way, but I promise you, I'm working on it. We can do therapy, anything that you need. Anything that would make you feel better."

"For Elijah?" she asks, pulling one hand away to bite at her cuticle, and I take it away, kissing the wound there.

"Not just for him. For us, too. I love you, Zoe. I'm still mad at you about what you did. I can't help that, but... I'm more miserable without you than I've ever been in my life," I say honestly. "Axel made me realize that being mad at you is one thing, but never having you in my life is quite another."

"You... you really want me? After what I did?" Zoe's voice was so shaky it is barely coherent.

"I want you. I want you so bad, Susie. Zoe. Baby blue. Anyone you are, anyone you might become, I want you. You and Elijah both.

She throws herself into my arms and I'm laughing and crying because I'm still angry and confused but I know this is what I want. I know this is what's right. Zoe was right all those years ago when she fell in love with me, even though I was too stupid to see it.

This is exactly how my life should end up, and I can't see the future. Maybe it'll go wrong. Maybe she'll leave me. Maybe nothing really does last forever.

But until my dying breath, I know I'll love Susie Zoe Carmichael, and that's all that matters.

Chapter 28

Zoe

The first year goes by in a blur. Jackson takes his own version of a paternity leave, telling Gemma she can't schedule a tour for at least two months. He says he deserves his time off just like Locke and Axel, and neither Gemma nor the guys complain. The band works on finishing recording their album and playing a few gigs in the area.

He spends every single day with Elijah, and when Elijah goes to school the year he turns five, Jackson's crying more than he is.

"I'll come back, daddy. Just like you did."

I can see Jackson near to losing it, so I carry Elijah out to the bus.

"He's so small," Jackson says weakly. "We should have taken him in the car. What if the other kids make fun of him?"

"Worrywart," I tell him, leaning up against him. "He wanted to ride the bus and he's going to be fine. Our guy is tough."

"He is," Jackson murmurs, but he's still staring after the bus.

"You know what this means, right?" I ask him, and Jackson stares at me, confused. I roll my eyes. "It means we get some adult time," I say, because with a kid who's a light sleeper, it's hard for us to keep up our usually vigorous sex life.

"Oh shit," Jackson gasps. "That's a perk I hadn't thought of."

"You gotta catch me first," I say, sprinting inside and up the stairs of the new house we'd moved into when Jackson and I got back together. He said Elijah deserved a yard to run around in, and he'd put a down payment on a house right away.

I love our house. I love my family. I love my life. I don't think that things can get any better.

Jackson doesn't attack me like usual, letting me kiss him and touch him and straddle his lap, tugging his shirt off. I frown a little, wondering why he isn't into it. Is he not attracted to me anymore?

"What's up?" I ask him, and he bites his lip.

"I'm a little nervous," he says, and I tilt my head.

"About Elijah? Baby, I keep telling you, he's going to be fine."

"You don't know that for sure." he mumbles.

"I know one thing for sure," I say, wrapping my arms around his neck.

"What's that?" he asks, kissing up my neck.

"I love you. I've been in love with you for most of my life.

"And I'm going to be in love with you for the rest of mine," he says softly, and Jackson can be so sweet, so gentle that I'm surprised when he flips me over, licking and biting at my neck. "And I want to put another baby in you," he finishes.

That's Jackson for you. My contradiction. A loyal man who takes care of everyone but forgets to take care of himself. A wonderful father. A gentle, loving soul who can also have the dirtiest mouth and the filthiest ideas in the bedroom. He loves me *and* he lusts for me, and sometimes, I wake up and think this has all been a dream.

It isn't a dream, though. It's the life we built, and I'm so happy I don't know what to do with myself. I don't think I can get happier until Elijah comes up the stairs one day, holding a little box in his hands.

Jackson's standing behind him, biting his lip like he's nervous.

"Daddy wanted me to ask you something," Elijah says, and I frown, picking him up.

Elijah struggles a little opening the box but he gets it done, and it's a beautiful sapphire ring because Jackson knows I hate diamonds.

"Daddy's using you so that I'll say yes," I say dryly, and Elijah nods, as if that's exactly what Jackson's told him.

"Did it work?" Jackson asks quietly, and I beam up at him.

"You could have asked me any way, and it would have worked. I can't wait to be your wife."

Jackson grins, that big, open smile that's always made me melt, and he and Elijah both hug-tackle me to the bed, beginning to tickle me.

* * *

Elijah is six the month we get married, three days after his birthday. He's excited, thinks it's the best birthday present he could have asked for.

Locke's the best man, with the rest of the Spades as groomsmen, and I have Gemma as my maid of honor (of course), and Harley and my sister as bridesmaids.

I sew my own dress, and it has a blue swatch cinching my waist and Jackson's wearing a black suit I tailored myself, with an old Van Halen T-shirt beneath instead of a button-up shirt. His hair hangs long and curling at the ends. He's let it grow out even more and he looks *gorgeous*.

I think I'm going to burst into tears before I get to him, but he's the one who's crying when I get there, murmuring to me how beautiful I look. I barely remember reciting my vows because I'm just stumbling over my words, looking into those deep green eyes that I've been wanting to drown in my whole life.

It's a princess story, isn't it? Maybe a rock princess story, because Jackson and the rest of the Spades perform a whole set at the reception and I have too much champagne and when he takes my garter off, it's with his teeth instead of his hand, of course.

We're not having a honeymoon because Jack and the Spades have gotten an international tour and their new album is selling extremely well, but we get one night in the honeymoon suite at the best hotel in town. Locke and Gemma buy us the room for a wedding gift.

Jackson carries me over the threshold and I'm tipsy and giggly and he kisses me hard before lying me down on the bed.

"God, Jackson, I love you."

Jackson grunts, spreading my thighs and kissing up my calves. "I love you too, baby blue."

I groan when he reaches my inner thighs, and he looks up at me before getting up on his knees, unbuttoning his slacks.

When he frees himself, I open my mouth in a big moan that whoever's staying next to us can probably hear. "I want you so much."

"Say it again," he commands, and I love it when he uses that tone of voice.

"I want you, Jackson," I say, and he leans down to bite my inner thigh, hard enough to leave a mark. I'm grinning because I know what he wants; I'm just being a brat.

"I love you, Jackson Arden," I say, just as he pushes inside me, and it's the truest thing I've ever said.

Thank you for reading Secret Baby For My Best Friend's Brother

If you loved this book, then you'll LOVE Unexpected Baby For My Brother's Best Friend...
Read on for a preview...

Chapter 29

Unexpected Baby For My Brother's Best Friend

I **broke the bro code and took my best friend's sister's V card.**
Now there's *hell* to pay.

Rock-n-roll and relationships don't mix.

I knew my best friend's sister was trouble, but I wanted a taste anyway.

I shouldn't be thinking about how her minidress would look crumpled on the floor.

Or how good she'd look on my bed.

Or the feeling of her thighs resting on my shoulders.

But it's all I can think about.

She's all I can think about.

One night of bliss may cost me everything.

My best friend, my career, and my carefree future.

But when she tells me I'm going to be her baby's daddy...

Continue to read Unexpected Baby For My Brother's Best Friend...

Chapter 1

Dylan

The soft music playing in the background as I write down the lyrics to my new song is my motivation. I always enjoy light upbeat tempo, and the bass guitar sounds. It is why I love *The Beatles*, regardless of how old-school modern-day rock bands consider them to be. They are my inspiration.

I was in the ninth grade when I first discovered my passion for music. It was also the year I met Lucas for the first time. A perfect guitarist and best wingman. Together, we grew up, made music, and had fun. It's funny how the best things in life happen when you least expect them. My journey with Lucas has been just that.

We are different in many ways, with music the one thing that makes us connect. But while Lucas enjoys the full life of our popularity and the benefits, I prefer to remain in the comfort of my room and make music.

"Hey D-man, come on." Speak of the devil. Glancing beyond the balcony of my suite, I spot him outside, along with his fiancée, Mika Robertson, and our band mates. They are all dressed for the beach and Mika is clinging to his arm, like always, as he is speaking to Chase and Jay.

Chapter 1

"Dylan, let's go," Lucas calls again, looking up at where I am. "You've been in there all day."

Resigned, I stand up and walk to the balcony so I don't have to shout. The smile on my face stays wide, but Lucas frowns at me. "You promised to make this trip fun," he complains.

"Yeah, D. You know what they say about all work no play, right? Get your ass down here and let's go!" Chase adds.

"Tonight, I promise. I just need to perfect some notes on the demo. Trust me, we'll rock and roll tonight." Winking at Mika, I add, "I promise, Mika. I know I owe you."

"Whatever, D-man." Jay dismisses me. Turning to the guys, he says, "I can only imagine what, or should I say *who* he is working on." Laughing, they turn and walk away. Always the prankster, that Jay. Shaking my head, I go back inside to the comfort of my solitude again.

Relief fills me as I sit on my chair, face the mirror, and begin practicing the lyrics for the demo.

"Late nights ... I love the late nights with you." The sound of my voice, the melody from my guitar, and my foot tapping on the ground bring the melody to light.

Perfecting my music is my life; it is all I can think of doing most of the time. And as much as I enjoy spending time with my friends, and especially hanging out with Lucas, making sure our band is successful is still the number one goal for me.

It's the only way I can have the platform to help the people who need a voice.

Also, I enjoy the golden silence of being alone. It helps me think ... helps me plan.

There's one note that's not quite right, yet, or I'm not quite hitting it. Groaning, I start from the beginning. Again.

Chapter 1

Taking my time to perfect the tone I want for the bridge of the song. Playing the guitar makes me feel alive, and as I approach the high rock part of the song, I feel my nerves settle inside me.

For years, my peace, my escape came from music. At fourteen, it was the one thing that kept me afloat. *"Your son's borderline depressed, and I think music keeps him going."*

Not like my mother cared what the therapist she was making me see twice a week thought when she came for a joint session. And she let me know just what she thought about it when we got home that day. She had two settings with me: caring mother for the public eye, and insults or just plain right ignoring me the rest of the time. I preferred when she ignored me. It hurt less.

The therapist had been right about so many things, but none of it mattered in the end, because when I reached fifteen, my mom said there was no need for the therapy sessions anymore. So, just as it had started, my therapy stopped. No regard for what I wanted or needed. It was never about that.

Playing at the back-alley club down the street where we lived in San Jose became my new therapy. I didn't need to listen to my mother's constant nagging, the loud noises when my parents got into a fight, or the harsh words whenever she was in one of her moods, as Dad called them.

I found solace at that bar. With Lucas, Jay, and Chase, I found my happy place.

Music.

I can't imagine doing anything else. At seventeen, when I moved out of my parents' house, my father finally found the courage to ask for a divorce. I suspected my mother would put up a fight, like she always did when she wanted to have her way, but none came.

Their divorce had been silent. Papers were signed, and I never had to see her again. Neither did my father. It had been all over. And yet, fifteen years later, I'm still somewhat that little boy who hated loud sounds and raised voices. Ironic considering my line of work, but when I'm singing and playing, my mind is somewhere else. However, I rarely ever enjoy hanging out in bars.

My cell phone buzzes on the table, distracting me from my thoughts, and I pick it up. "Ken," I say as I rub the back of my neck. "How's it going?"

"Great," Ken Daystar, our manager, and number one fan, answers in a light tone. "Lucas and the others?"

"Having fun someplace at the beach," I reply.

"And you? Who do you have beside you right now? Blonde or redhead?"

I laugh at Ken's question, then shake my head and stroke my jaw. Ken thinks I'm a major player. That I am always with a different girl anytime I'm not with the guys. I don't correct his assumptions.

"Blonde," I reply, glancing at the poster of Gwen Stefani on my wall. She is my number one celebrity crush and blonde as can be, so it's not like I'm lying.

"Great, don't forget, two weeks and we need you back for the tour," Ken says. "With Lucas out on his honeymoon, we will need you to cover for him for a couple of shows. Think that will work?"

The plan is for Lucas to join us by the time we get to Wyoming. With me as the lead guitar player and second voice, I usually leave the lead singing to him. Not having him there means I'm stuck as lead singer and lead guitar since Chase is our drummer and Jay plays the bass.

Double the fun for me, right?

He doesn't give me time to answer. "Either way, congratulate Lucas for me. I should join you all on the island before the wedding."

"Will do, talk later."

He drops the call, and I drop my phone on the table, place my guitar on the bed, then rub the back of my neck. Rising to my feet, I stretch my muscles for a bit to release the cramps starting to build up on my shoulders.

Guess I should join the others. I take off my shirt and walk to my bathroom for a quick shower.

* * *

Lucas and Mika excuse themselves and leave. Jay and Chase left earlier to go to a club they heard was pumping nearby. Those two are party animals. I'm nursing my third glass of brandy, the same one I had just started when the happy couple decided to call it a night, enjoying the light music in the bar, and thinking it is time to call it quits too when a group of people walks in. *Guess the night is just starting for some people.*

My eyes immediately land on two girls coming in. Specifically a woman with dirty blonde hair waving down her back and a killer smile. She is facing my way, and I'm blown away by the sparkle in her eyes.

A rush of adrenaline suddenly flows through me. Though beautiful women are always surrounding us when we play, that doesn't make me appreciate true beauty any less. And unfortunately, no matter how I act, as soon as they find out what I do for a living, they always have one impression of me.

Playboy.

Regardless of how nice or how rough I act, though, they love the attention they can get from hanging out around me. Which is not surprising either. Women are fickle. I often wonder how people manage to find just one to stick with.

And it's not that I have a thing against commitment, love, or big weddings. Lucas is all in that scene and I am happy for him. I can tell he loves Mika very much, and I like her too because she is one of the few good women I have met, but that's just it.

Besides Mika and Carol, Lucas's mom, I never keep any other women around long enough to know what they are like. We meet, have a fun time together, and on they go.

I respect them and admire them, but that is it. There is no point in losing myself, like my father did, or risking the heartbreak that comes with it.

It's not worth it.

So, I always keep a clear head. I'm always honest about how things are, and we keep things simple and easy. I empty my glass and stand up. I can't take my eyes off this blonde.

She laughs again. Somehow, her deep timbre reaches me and it's like every other noise around me fades away. Like a parched man to water, I can't stop myself from following the sound. As I draw closer, the woman sitting to her side stands and walks away. The blonde casts a glance over her shoulder, and her eyes briefly land on mine.

That single moment is enough to get my pulse racing and my heart thundering in my chest. It is an intense response; one I have never felt.

"No wonder the sky is dark outside," I say as I take the empty stool next to hers and order for the waiter. "All the color is in your eyes." My voice is a low, deep baritone that sounds husky even to me, but it doesn't matter because I love the tingles already racing through me when she gives me a side grin.

"That's a cheesy pick-up line," she says and looks at me again.

God, I love her eyes and her smile.

She is gorgeous. The perfect set of white teeth flashes at me. I notice the small button nose on her face and the way her brows arch softly as her eyes flicker over mine.

"You think so? I should try again, then," I answer, and she laughs.

"I was wondering if you were an artist because you were drawing me in," I say cheekily. She laughs.

"Wait. I have another one. We are not socks, but we'd still make a great pair. How's that?" I lay it on really thick, with a smile on my lips.

"That's so bad," she replies, still laughing. "Does that work for you?"

"Every time," I say. "I mean it, though," I add when she laughs again. "I can't take my eyes off you. I think it's your eyes ... or maybe your smile. Either way, you're the most beautiful woman I have seen here tonight."

Her laugh mesmerizes me for a second. The effect is even stronger at close range and I can't help but feel like I have superpowers for making her laugh so much in just these couple of minutes.

"Tonight, huh? I see. Do you keep a tally every night?"

"Oh, no. This is definitely a special night," I play along. She has spunk and I find I'm even more intrigued by the beauty before me.

"Oh yeah? And what's so special about tonight?"

"You're here." And I thank the rock gods that I decided to join my friends tonight.

"Flattering," she says. "I like it. And I like you."

197

She turns back to the table and picks up her glass. The waiter arrives in front of us then, and I ask her, "Let me buy you a drink, and then you can tell me what your story is."

"What makes you think I have one?"

"You're at a bar, drinking alone ... It's either, you're done with one relationship or you're scouting for another."

The waiter pours us a drink and I down mine in one go. She does the same, and orders for another. I discreetly notice the rings on her fingers. Her hands are slender, her nails a hot, red shade that makes my blood start to hum with a low wave of desire as I imagine them scratching down my back while I make her scream my name.

"Are *you* scouting for another?" she asks me. When she looks at me again, her round eyes latch onto mine. There is something so intense about her gaze that a shiver races up my spine. I just can't explain it, but I sense the fire in her instantly.

The corners of my lips lift into a smile, and I shake my head. "Not at all," I say. "That's the last thing on my mind tonight.... You?"

She hesitates. I wish I knew what she's thinking because her eyes get clouded. I find myself leaning into her without even realizing it, and one more breath brings in her scent. It is intoxicating. My body comes alive and a dance of raw hunger starts inside of me.

My eyes drop to her lips. They are full, soft, and inviting. I can already imagine myself tasting them.

"No," she answers, and I pull myself back to reality and look into her eyes again. "I'm not looking for one either. Not tonight."

Continue to read Unexpected Baby For My Brother's Best Friend...

Chapter 2

Amy

He has the most captivating eyes ever. His smile and small hand gestures as he talks suck up my attention. I am lost in his eyes and drowning in the sound of his voice. I instantly know this is the man I came looking for tonight.

As I sit here with him and let him pour me another drink, I remember Casey's advice to me before she ditched me for some random guy some minutes back.

Try to have fun, Amy ... It's a vacation, and you work too hard. Loosen up, get laid, maybe. I remember Casey's giggle before she left me. As if I could afford to take any time off. This might be a vacation spot, but other than the wedding party, this is business as usual for me. I'm here to work first and enjoy the island second. But then her words, *Get laid,* come back again as I look at the man before me, leaving me shuddering at the mere thought of some action with this guy. Casey thinks I've been with a few guys, but truth is, I haven't found anyone who made me want to go all the way. I have fooled around, of course. And been in a few relationships. But when push comes to shove, I have never been

Chapter 2

able to just let go and give myself to anyone. So, here I am, at twenty-two and still a virgin. How sad is that?

I look at him then, and he is staring at my lips. The first thing that crosses my mind is panic. Would I really be able to give myself away to a stranger? Even if it is this god before me?

I came here to Hawaii, regardless of the workload I have right now, for my brother's wedding. Both he and his fiancée made me promise to show up, and as the designer for the wedding dress and the groom's sister, how could I not? But the truth is, I would have preferred to avoid my mother. She is a bit too much. And now, with this wedding, I know I will never hear the end of her disappointment—that I am yet to bring any man home, or even a date for the day—all of which I am used to. Sheesh, you'd think I'm going on forty the way she talks sometimes.

My brother was always the golden boy. Mom loves him, Dad was proud of him, and it is difficult being my own person without the tag... *My brother's sister.*

I used to hate it when everyone addressed me in association with him, but with time, I learned to get over it. Making my own name and being my own person is all I want to do now, and designing this wedding dress is a huge deal for me because it can give me the exposure I need.

My fashion brand, Keaton Designs, is solely me. Keaton is my late granddad's name. He was my favorite person in the world and I was his. He always made me feel special. To him, I was always the light that shone brighter. Too bad we lost him so soon.

Shaking myself out of it, I look at the man in front of me again, and I decide maybe I can be bold and stupid for once and do something Casey would do.

"First time in Hawaii?" I ask him.

He immediately shakes his head. "Third."

"Wow, they say the third time is a charm, right? Have you found yours yet?"

The way he looks at me after that question sends a shiver down my spine. I can't tell what it is about this man that gets to me. Can it be the perfect shape of his face? Long, light brown hair tied to the back of his head, or his eyes that are a forest green shade? Or is it that voice?

It is smooth and yet terrifying. It makes my skin flush and tingle, and he hasn't even touched me yet. He lifts a hand to pick up the bottle the waiter left for us, and I move to pick up my glass at the same time. Our fingers brush and his touch on my skin lingers.

The slow hum rising in the pit of my stomach sends my pulse into a pounding rage. My nerves immediately flair. I have never felt anything like this.

"I think I found one," he says, then picks up his glass and winks at me before drinking.

My heartbeat triples and knocks the wind out of my lungs. I drink too. The fiery liquid burns a path down my throat and the impact on my head is intense.

"It's my first time in Hawaii," I tell him, then set my glass on the table. "I'm here for a wedding."

"Crazy, I'm here for one too. My best friend found his love match and they are perfect for each other."

"That sounds nice," I say.

"It does. I love that he is happy."

"But?" I ask, sensing there is more he wants to say.

He cocks a brow. "No buts."

When he doesn't add anything, I raise my left brow suspiciously.

"I mean it," he says with a smile. "No buts. I genuinely

love that he is happy. I'm not some sucker who believes people can't fall in love."

"I am not either," I say, but keep my eyes on him. We stare at each other for a second and he laughs at the exact same time I burst out laughing.

"I know what you're thinking," he says, and points a finger at me. "You think I'm a playboy who doesn't think he can fall in love."

"Aren't you?' I ask. "I mean, here's one thing. The hair," I say with a hand demonstrating. "That tattoo that says, 'For the love of man,' which sounds sexist, by the way, and then there's that smile, the rings ... Everything about you screams I'd get my heart broken."

He laughs harder. "But that's only if you're looking for love. Are you?"

"No," I answer. Love is the last thing I want right now. I still have a lot to accomplish. This year, I plan to strike one major milestone and get my designs on a top fashion show like New York or Paris. Then I have to travel for shoots and deals. Love is down at the bottom of my list.

"But I'll want it someday, won't you?"

He seems to think for a second before he shrugs. "Let's just say I'm not out searching."

Our eyes meet again, and I have the feeling there is more to that story, but I say nothing.

Not my concern.

"What's with that shirt?" I ask, laughing as I point at it, letting the topic go so we can move on to lighter topics.

* * *

Time goes by unnoticed, and the bar starts to get emptier and emptier. Still, we sit there, laughing and drinking. We talk about anything and everything until he tells me about his passion for music. I can imagine him singing on a stage. His voice is lovely even when he speaks.

"Sing for me," I ask, but he shakes his head.

"You'd have to do something for me in return," he answers. I hesitate and he quickly adds, "Don't worry, it's not difficult."

"What is it?"

"Maybe I should get your word and sing first so you can't back out later," he says.

I giggle again and I press a hand to my lips. For some reason, I can't stop laughing and smiling with him.

"Alright, I'll tell you what it is first." He sighs theatrically, then shifts back on his chair. "Let me take you someplace nice tonight. I know a great spot near the beach. It's only past midnight and it's the perfect time to go there."

"You think so?" I ask.

He nods. "I promise I'll sing when we get there."

"Fine." I don't need to think twice.

Standing up, I reach for my purse, but when he puts his hand on mine, I freeze. His skin is not cool like I thought it would be. It's hot, and the warmth seeps through my skin. My fingers curl even before he tightens his grip around them and places a dollar bill on the table.

The waiter gives him a small salute as he is leading me toward the exit.

Once outside, he pulls me to a power bike and takes out some keys from his pocket. "Ever ridden one of these?"

"Yes, my brother used to have one," I reply as he hands me a helmet. I secure it on my head and wait for him to climb first.

"Hold on tight," he says to me, and my hands instinctively tighten around his midsection. Feeling the hard muscles of his rock-solid abdomen, I lick my suddenly dry lips.

My pulse starts racing again, and there's a fluttering movement inside me. The leather and wood scent combination wrecks my senses. I imagine what it would be like to touch his bare skin.

The leather jacket he is wearing is cool against my cheek as I press it onto his back. He kicks the engine of his bike alive in one start, swerves, and enters the road.

We ride for a while, and the entire time, I am melting inside. When he finally slows his ride at the beach, I get off and he takes my hand again.

He leads me toward the small stand at a distance. There is a crowd of people there, some people seated, others dancing. A band is playing, and though the music is loud, lots of laughter and the cool wind of the night make everything more charming.

"What's going on?" I ask at the top of my voice because I can barely hear myself.

He grins as he turns to me and says, "It's a live band for hula dancing."

"Hula?"

He does a small movement with his hips and hands in front of him, and oh boy, I can't hold back my laugh. He looks funny and sexy at the same time.

Cheeks wide from all the grinning, I ask. "Who taught you that?"

"It's Hawaii, everyone loves to dance," he says, then takes my hand and leads me to the dance floor.

We spend the next twenty minutes dancing and I have no idea what I'm doing. I'm just moving my hips and legs to match his rhythm and having too much fun. The best fun I have had in a while.

Chapter 2

"Okay, I'll sing now," he says and walks to the stage. He says something to the lead singer, and they give him the mic. Then he turns and points in my direction. "This one is for you."

He starts to sing a slow song, and my heart warms as I listen to his melodious voice. The warmth spreads through me, and I love the feeling. When he ends the song, as the crowd cheers and claps for him. He comes back to my side and we sit.

"That was amazing," I tell him.

"Thank you."

We stay on the beach for a long time, just enjoying the weather, the vibe, the night. Each other. As soon as the crowd starts to disperse, I realize I drank too much. I am laughing hard as I hold onto his hand and stroll with him toward his bike.

The night's wind is heavy now, probably because we are at the beach. When he faces me as we get to his bike, the wind ruffles my hair and makes it fly all over my face.

I laugh and use both hands to arrange it. He reaches out to help me, and the minute he touches my face, something tenses in the air around us. His eyes are on mine again, and there's this magnetic pull. My blood starts to hum to the tune of desire stirring inside me, and I feel myself floating away even before his lips touch mine.

His kiss is cool, and it is the best thing I have ever tasted. His tongue sweeps over my lips and makes me shiver. Who knew a kiss could feel like this? His hands move around my waist, and he pulls me to him. I part for him and give in to the sensations wracking through me.

As his hands move up and down my back, I press into him. The stir of his erection makes me yank my lips from his. I am panting and so is he, and he is staring deep into my eyes again.

Oh, the warmth surrounding me is unbearable. I've never been with anyone like this before. No man has stirred any feelings as powerful as this. That's why it was easy for me to focus on my career and school before that. That is why I was able to stay away from boys my age. But that's just it. This is not a boy, this is a man. All man. And I want to lose control and let myself go for one night because this man is *that* exciting.

He kisses me again and I can't deny the passion it stirs in me. His taste is addicting. The blend of rum and brandy on his lips steals every logical sense of reasoning I have left.

"The beach has a suite," he is saying as he drags his lips down to the side of my neck and feasts on the pulse there. I arch for him, giving him better access. His kisses leave me shivering.

"Hm?" I can't even form words.

"There's a suite on the beach."

I can finally make sense of what he is saying to me.

"I know," I say, but my voice is husky, and I can barely hear myself. Not sure if he heard me, I nod, moan, and then nibble on my lower lip.

He takes my hand and leads me in the direction of the magnificent building to our left. Once we get inside, he gets a key for us from the reception, and leads me upstairs. Everything is happening so fast I don't even have the time to question if I'm doing the right thing. Your first time is a big deal, but this feels so right. To be here with him now. And then the time for thinking is over because as soon as the door shuts behind us, I'm in his arms again and what was still left of my brain shuts down.

His lips dip and take mine for another kiss that leaves

me breathless. Nothing else matters as I slip my hands under his shirt and touch the hard muscles of his chest.

This is it. I'm really doing this. My first time. And this is going to be the best night ever!

Continue to read Unexpected Baby For My Brother's Best Friend...

Printed in Great Britain
by Amazon